PUFFIN BOOKS

The Runaways

Praise for Megan Rix

'If you love Michael Morpurgo, you'll enjoy this' *Sunday Express*

'A moving tale told with warmth, kindliness and lashings of good sense that lovers of Dick King-Smith will especially appreciate' *The Times*

'Every now and then a writer comes along with a unique way of storytelling. Meet Megan Rix . . . her novels are deeply moving and will strike a chord with animal lovers' *LoveReading*

'A perfect story for animal lovers and lovers of adventure stories' Travelling Book Company

Praise from Megan's young readers:

'I never liked reading until one day I was in Waterstones and I picked up some books. One was . . . called *The Bomber Dog*. I loved it so much I couldn't put it down' Luke, 8

'I found this book amazing' Nayah, 11

'EPIC BOOK!!!' Jessica, 13

'One of my favourite books' Chloe, Year 8

MEGAN RIX is the recent winner of the Stockton and Shrewsbury Children's Book Awards, and has been shortlisted for numerous other children's book awards. She lives with her husband by a river in England. When she's not writing she can be found walking her golden retrievers, Traffy and Bella, who are often in the river.

Books by Megan Rix

THE BOMBER DOG

THE GREAT ESCAPE

THE HERO PUP

THE RUNAWAYS

A SOLDIER'S FRIEND

THE VICTORY DOGS

www.meganrix.com

The
Runaways

megan rix

PUFFIN

PUFFIN BOOKS

UK | USA | Canada | Ireland | Australia
India | New Zealand | South Africa

Puffin Books is part of the Penguin Random House group of companies
whose addresses can be found at global.penguinrandomhouse.com.

puffinbooks.com

Penguin
Random House
UK

First published 2015
001

Text copyright © Megan Rix, 2015
Map copyright © David Atkinson, 2015
Illustrations copyright © Puffin Books, 2015
Illustrations by Becky Morrison

The moral right of the author and illustrators has been asserted

Set in 13/20 pt by Baskerville MT Std
Typeset by Jouve (UK), Milton Keynes
Printed in Great Britain by Clays Ltd, St Ives plc

A CIP catalogue record for this book is available from the British Library

ISBN: 978-0-141-35764-5

www.greenpenguin.co.uk

*An elephant's call that is silent to humans may be
heard by another elephant more than six miles away.*

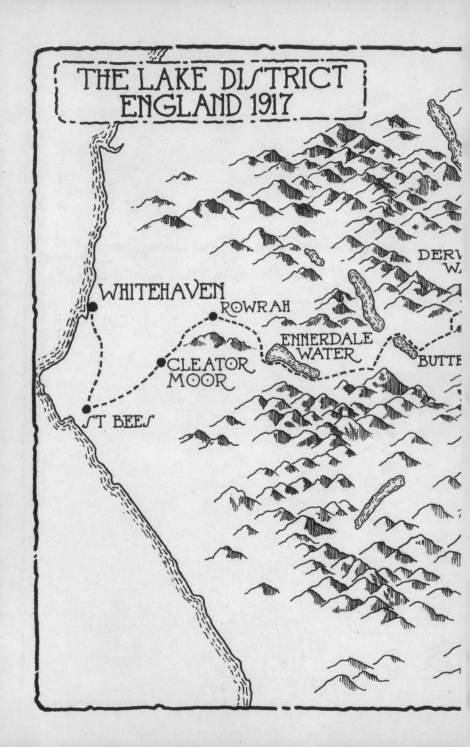

Chapter 1

Harvey always wore the turquoise ruff around his furry black-and-white neck for the show. So when he saw the baby elephant heading towards him, intent on pulling it off as she'd managed to do the day before, he skittered away from her before she got a chance.

Tara gave a trumpeting *squee* as she headed after the Border collie across the elephant tent. But Harvey was too old and wily to be caught by a two-year-old elephant and he hid under the oversized props they sometimes used in the act. Tara knelt down and stretched out her trunk as far as it would go, but hard as she tried she couldn't reach him. Finally she gave a trumpet of frustration, headed back to her mother, Shanti, and had some milk instead.

Drink over, the baby elephant watched from the other side of the tent as fifteen-year-old Albert, dressed in a turquoise 'Arabian Nights' elephant trainer's costume, carefully combed his hair in front of the full-length mirror. Harvey poked his pointy nose under one of the props and watched Tara watching Albert.

Deep in thought, Albert put the comb back in his pocket and didn't pay attention to the little elephant as she pottered over to him.

Tara stuck out her trunk and ruffled his just-combed fair hair.

'Tara!' he said, pulling out the comb again and quickly smoothing his hair back down. 'You can be a little minx sometimes!'

Tara gave a joyful *squee* that sounded almost like a giggle. Not sorry at all. As soon as he'd finished combing his hair, she went to mess it up again, but this time her mother stopped her with her trunk and a warning noise.

Albert felt sorry for the elephants. In the wild they'd be able to wander wherever they liked. Tara would have other elephants to play with and probably a watering hole or a river to splash in rather than the bucket of water that was all he could manage to give her. He always treated the elephants with kindness, unlike some trainers he'd heard about. But, nevertheless, they spent most of their days and nights tied up in their tent, apart from when they were performing for the public in the big top.

He really couldn't blame Tara for wanting to play or for being mischievous. She was bored. He knew that the circus wasn't the right place for the elephants to be, but he tried to make it the best place for them that he could. Maybe their new home would be better. He hoped so.

'Here, Shanti, let's put this on you,' Albert said, picking up the multicoloured headdress the Asian elephant wore during the show. It had been made especially for her and had her name embroidered across the star in the centre.

Shanti bowed her giant head so he could tie the headdress behind her ears. She'd been part of circus life from the time she was five years old and she was now twenty-two.

'You look beautiful,' he told the sweet-natured, gentle elephant as he pressed his face into her warm, rough skin and ran his hand down her trunk. Shanti made a soft rumbling sound.

Tara, however, did not help Albert like her mother had done. As soon as she saw him pick up her own much smaller headdress she turned round so her bottom was facing him instead of her face. When Albert walked round to the front of her she made a noise that sounded very much like a giggle and turned round the other way.

'Come on, Tara, you know you have to wear it,' he told her. He didn't want them to be late for their very last show.

But Tara only shook her head and backed away as he stepped towards her. They'd played this game before.

Harvey came out from under the props and looked from one to the other, his tail wagging.

'Hmm,' said Albert, putting his hand in his pocket and acting as if he didn't care a bit what Tara did. He pulled out an apple, one of Tara's favourite treats, and Tara stretched out her trunk, wanting to take the apple from him.

Albert looked at the apple in one hand and then he looked at Tara's headdress in his other hand and waggled it. Tara knew exactly what she needed to do if she wanted the apple.

She stood quietly in front of Albert and let him put on her headdress with her name embroidered across the star like her mum's.

'That's a good elephant,' Albert said, giving her a stroke. Tara's skin was much less rough and a lot more furry than Shanti's. She even had a tuft of fur on the top her head that gave her an impish look. It matched her personality, he thought.

Albert bit into the apple and shared the bitten pieces between the little elephant and Shanti. Harvey barked and nudged Albert with his nose.

'Don't worry, I haven't forgotten you.' Albert smiled at the old dog. 'There's a bone for you, but not till after the show.'

Albert checked himself one last time in the mirror before they left the tent. It was the last time he'd wear the sparkling turquoise elephant trainer's outfit before he set off for the front. The last time for, well he didn't exactly know quite how long, that he, Shanti, Tara and Harvey would perform together.

When the war started in August 1914 his father had said it would be over by Christmas. Everyone thought it would be done and dusted in a few months. But it was now September 1917 and the war was still going on, only his dad wasn't around any more to see the end of it. Thinking about how much he missed him made Albert feel sad. At least his father had got to see Tara being born before he died and Albert was glad about that. It had always been very important to his dad that Shanti was happy and no mum could have been happier with her baby than Shanti was. Not many people get to see a newborn elephant, and Tara had looked so sweet as she took her first wobbly steps while Shanti stood protectively over her. For a long time she hid under her mum's tummy whenever she was scared or worried about anything.

'But you don't seem to be scared of much these days, do you? More like full of mischief and fun!' he told the baby elephant as she stretched out her trunk towards his head and he ducked back from her before she could mess up his hair again.

The band started to play, which meant the matinee audience must be seated. It was time to go on.

Albert still felt nervous before each performance even though he knew no one was really watching him. The audience only had eyes for the elephants, and that was just the way it should be, in Albert's opinion. Shanti and Tara were the most beautiful, majestic and just downright magical creatures he could ever imagine, and he wanted to share their grace with everyone.

Harvey pushed his head under Albert's hand and Albert stroked him.

'Come on then, one last show. Let's make it a good one,' Albert said, as they headed for the big top. 'Tails!' he instructed, and Tara held on to Shanti's tail as she was supposed to do. Shanti, as always, took the lead, with Harvey bringing up the rear.

The band was playing a new tune now.

Harvey panted as he waited to go into the ring.

'Wait for it,' Albert told him, as he looked round the tent flap at the afternoon's audience.

Those who'd paid the most for their seats got to sit on the comfortable maroon velvet padded chairs at the front. But there were only two people sitting in those seats today. A middle-aged woman with her brown hair tied in a bun, and a suited man in a hat sitting beside her.

The rest of the audience at Whitehaven was pitifully small. Maybe twelve in total on the cheaper bench seats. Six of those were voluntary nurses in uniform, plus a soldier and his girlfriend and three children with their mum.

Albert bit his bottom lip. Not enough people to keep an elephant in cabbages; certainly not enough to pay a whole circus crew. Not that they had a proper crew any more. Most of the younger men had enlisted already. The circus was on its knees and couldn't go on. This matinee wasn't just the last show for Albert, the elephants and Harvey. It was the last show for everyone else in the circus too.

The ringmaster, Jedediah Lewis, was in the centre of the ring. He whisked off his top hat, raised it in the air, and shouted, 'And now for your delight and entertainment, at great expense, all the way from the jungle . . .'

As the first note of the popular 'Royal Decree' march was banged out by the band, Harvey gave a small whine and put out his paw.

Albert pulled back the tent flap and the three animals ran into the circus ring. As Albert went past the maroon chairs, he heard the woman say:

'Now we're in for a treat.'

'Whatever you say, Beatrix,' the man told her as he checked his pocket watch.

The animals paraded round until the music changed to a tinkling lullaby and then, quick as a flash, Harvey jumped into the pram that Albert pushed into the ring. Shanti curled her trunk round the oversized handle, and as 'Rock-a-bye Baby' continued to play she rocked the pram back and forth as if she were lulling a baby to sleep. Meanwhile, Tara took the giant-sized baby's bottle that Albert held out to her. It was filled with water that she tipped into her mouth.

Albert glanced over as the scant audience *ooohed*, *aaahed* and clapped. His eyes widened as he watched a red-faced, broken-nosed man sit down at the back of the bench seats. What on earth was Carl from Cullen's Circus doing here? There was bad blood between Albert's family and Cullen's Circus where Carl worked as the elephant trainer. Shanti had come from there and the last time Albert's father had seen Carl he'd been so angry with his cruel treatment of her that there had almost been a fight. But what was Carl doing at the Lewis Brothers' show?

Albert looked back at the animals as the audience gasped and pointed at Tara. So far the little elephant had never squirted the water from the giant baby's bottle at the audience. But she'd squirted it at the ringmaster only the day before. Jedediah had been furious, until he'd heard the delighted audience's reaction. Always a showman, his angry face had changed to beaming smiles as he took a bow. Then he waggled his finger at Tara who lifted her trunk and gave her distinctive high-pitched trumpet in response. That had made the small audience laugh even more.

Albert knew the ringmaster wanted Tara to squirt the water at him again today, but instead she pointed her trunk in Harvey's direction, as she'd been taught to do, but not too close because Harvey wasn't fond of water.

Now, when Harvey saw what Tara was about to do, he jumped out of the pram and ran around the ring. *Good boy, just as we practised*, thought Albert. Harvey never let him down. Tara turned in a circle, her trunk pointing after him as he ran. But, just before she did finally spray the water, Harvey jumped back into the pram and Shanti used her trunk to pull down the hood so he'd be protected. The audience clapped and clapped.

Next, Albert threw an oversized football into the ring and Tara dropped the bottle, ran over to it and started to push it along with her trunk. Harvey jumped out of the pram and managed to stand on top of the ball before Albert blew the whistle and Harvey jumped off again. Shanti picked the ball up with her trunk and threw it across the circus ring into the goal that Albert had just placed there, as both Tara and Harvey ran after it.

When the game of football was over, the band struck up and the elephants and dog paraded round the ring once more, only at a slower pace now, in time with the familiar music. Shanti waved a giant-sized Union Jack flag, Tara swished a twenty-foot-long yellow ribbon around her, and Harvey, wearing a miniature soldier's cap, walked on his hind legs before running up Shanti's back to sit behind her head. The audience applauded and Albert smiled, swelling with pride.

Albert glanced over at the benches. Carl was gone and Albert was glad. His attention was pulled back to the show as Tara gave one last trumpet as she made her way out of the ring to the sound of the 'Pomp and Circumstance' march. Shanti raised her trunk in a wave of goodbye, and Harvey followed the elephants out of the ring.

'A big round of applause for our amazing elephants and their dog friend . . .' The ringmaster's voice faded as Albert, Shanti, Tara and Harvey left the big top.

Once they were outside, Harvey looked up at Albert and wagged his tail.

'Good boy,' Albert said, giving him a scratch behind the ears. 'I'm going to miss all this.' But most of all he was going to miss Harvey and the elephants.

Back in the tent, the woman on the maroon chair said, 'I really should write a story about a circus.'

'Bit of a change from bunnies,' said the man.

'Not if it's a guinea-pig circus,' she smiled.

The six volunteer nurses clapped and clapped.

'I love that baby elephant . . .'

'What a character . . .'

'The "Pomp and Circumstance" march makes me think of our boys at the front,' one of the nurses said, dabbing at her eyes with a handkerchief.

'No tears, now,' another of the nurses said firmly, as she smoothed down her new apron.

'That won't help our soldiers once we're over in France, will it?'

The nurse shook her head.

'A cheery face then, that's what they need.'

The nurse with the handkerchief sniffed.

'I heard they were going to use more elephants on the farms to help out with the ploughing,' another of the nurses said as two clowns came running into the ring.

'Really?' said the apron nurse.

'Well, Lizzie the Sheffield elephant has been a great success for Tommy Ward's scrap metal business, hauling scrap metal and munitions across the city. I was reading in the newspaper about her helping herself to a carter's lunch just the other day.'

'No reason why a farm elephant shouldn't work out well too,' the handkerchief nurse said, and the other nurses agreed as they settled down to watch the rest of the show.

Chapter 2

Forest View Farm's two gentle shire horses, Buttercup and Bluebell, had been taken by the army right at the start of the war, three years ago. The sergeant who took them told Mr Jones the farmer and his two children, Yolanda and AJ, that they needed strong horses at the front and everyone had to do their bit, even children.

AJ had been very worried when he'd heard this because he thought it might mean he had to go to war too, and he'd heard they had rats that were bigger than cats in the trenches.

'I don't like rats,' he told the sergeant, who just looked a bit confused.

Gradually all the shire horses, as well as just about every other type of horse, in Stony Oakhill village had been taken, apart from Old Ned and a few others who were too old to do any work any more.

The farmers and foresters asked the soldiers what they were supposed to do without their horses, but they had no answer for them.

On Mr Jones's farm they'd had to struggle on without the horses for nearly two years before Annie, from the Women's Land Army, had arrived with a steam logger to help them with the forestry. Yolanda had never seen a woman wearing trousers before and she was almost more impressed by the sight of Annie, who couldn't have been more than sixteen years old, than she was by the logger. Annie just seemed so free and she always said just exactly what she was thinking. Yolanda wished she could be more like her.

'Don't worry, this can do the work of ten horses,' Annie told AJ and Yolanda from the top of the noisy smelly thing.

And maybe it could have done if the army hadn't requisitioned it too a few weeks later!

'Now what are we supposed to do?' Annie said in dismay, pushing back her wide-brimmed hat with the Women's Land Army badge on it, as she watched the steam logger being taken away.

'Our dad'll think of something,' Yolanda told her confidently. Ever since their mum had died, Yolanda had taken over most of the household chores. Not that she minded, not at all, what with Dad being in a wheelchair. But despite that he managed pretty well, and he loved solving problems. She told Annie how he'd got the blacksmith to adapt his wheelchair so it had bigger, thicker wheels than normal wheelchairs and could go on the grass and around the farm more easily.

'He had the handles raised and a bar put across the back so it's easier for people of different heights to push it,' AJ said.

'And a harness so Noodle, my donkey, could pull it too,' Yolanda added. 'Not that he's here to do any pulling now.'

Although she missed Buttercup and Bluebell badly, she missed Noodle and his braying even more. But the army sergeant had said they needed him too and so off to war he'd gone shortly after the horses.

'Well, someone had better think of something,' Annie said. Even with the help of the Land Army girls, the farms were struggling to survive.

Then, one morning in August, their dad was reading aloud to them from the newspaper about Lizzie, an elephant who worked in Sheffield.

'*Yesterday evening Lizzie was pulling the heavy factory cart when she saw a boy's cap that she thought looked tasty, and quick as a wink the cap was gone . . .*'

'I wish we could have an elephant like Lizzie,' ten-year-old AJ said with a laugh.

'Me too,' said Yolanda, as she poured more tea in her father's cup.

'Of course,' their father said, slamming the newspaper down on the breakfast table. 'That's it!'

'What's it?' Yolanda had asked, as AJ took a desperate swig of milk to wash away the piece of bread that he'd choked on in shock at the newspaper slamming.

'The answer to our problem,' their dad said as he looked over at AJ. 'You OK?'

AJ nodded and swallowed hard.

'What's the answer?' asked Yolanda. Although she didn't even know what the question was.

'We'll get an elephant of our own.'

Yolanda and AJ looked at each other in amazement.

'An elephant?' AJ squeaked.

'If it's good enough for Sheffield, it's good enough for us. It can do the heavy lifting work that the horses used to do and be a huge help to the farms and the forest. I don't know why I didn't think of it before. When your mother and I helped to run your grandad's tea plantation in Ceylon, we saw adult elephants doing lots of different jobs.'

'But how will we get an elephant?' Yolanda asked. It wasn't like they were growing on trees in the Lake District.

Mr Jones tapped the newspaper on the table. 'We'll put an advert in the paper and see if anyone has one for sale,' he said.

And that's what they did. And in fact not one but two circuses came forward. Mr Jones went with the one that would be in Cumbria the soonest because they didn't want to wait too long.

'We're really, really getting an elephant?' Yolanda said, in disbelief.

'Yes,' said her dad. 'Her name's Shanti, which means peaceful.'

AJ hoped their elephant wouldn't get too hungry and accidentally eat his cap like Lizzie had done – or other bits of him, come to that.

The news of the elephant coming quickly spread throughout their village and the surrounding ones too.

'Your dad's crazy thinking an elephant can help us,' said Joseph, who was in Yolanda and AJ's class at the village school. Most of the other children agreed with him. 'I don't think *my* dad would think it was a very good idea.'

AJ was about to tell Joseph he was wrong, but Yolanda gave him a nudge under the table.

Joseph's dad and older brother were fighting on the Western Front. AJ remembered their dad had said they had to be especially kind to anyone whose family members were fighting in the war.

'I'm going to join the army too as soon as I'm old enough. As long as the war's not over by then,' Joseph continued, sounding a bit worried that it might be.

Mr Soames, their teacher, heard him.

'I'm sure you'll make an excellent addition to any army, Joseph,' he said wryly.

Joseph sat up very tall on the long bench seat as if he were already imagining himself as a military man.

'Did you hear about Mr Jones's elephant, sir?' he asked the teacher.

'A whisper might have reached my ears. I think it's reached just about everyone's ears,' Mr Soames said with a twinkle in his eye.

'My mum says Mr Jones would be better off buying more crops and sheep and food for the tenant farmers than wasting it on a great beast that'll probably trample us all to death while we sleep,' said Mary.

'Did she?' Mr Soames said mildly, and he turned to the large globe on his desk. 'Who can tell me where elephants come from?'

'The circus?'

'Travelling zoos?'

'Where they originally come from?' Mr Soames sighed.

'Africa.'

'Asia.'

'India.'

'Ceylon,' AJ added, thinking about what his dad had told him.

'And what's the difference between an African and an Asian elephant?' Mr Soames asked.

'One of them's got bigger ears, sir.'

'Like you, Dobbin,' said the boy next to him flicking his ear.

'Ow!'

'The African does indeed have larger ears than the Asian elephant,' said Mr Soames.

'The Asian elephants are supposed to be a bit gentler,' Yolanda said. 'That's what Dad told us.'

'He also said they put strings of dried chillies near the crops to stop them getting eaten or trampled on by the elephants,' said AJ. 'Elephants hate chillies.'

'What do elephants like to eat?' Mr Soames asked everyone.

'Vegetables and fruit.'

'Schoolboys' caps,' AJ said, thinking of Lizzie the elephant.

Mr Soames shook his head, smiling.

'Peanuts.'

'Our dad says that's not true.'

'And who knows how much they drink?'

'A lot.'

'One large bathtub full of water every day,' said AJ.

'No! They can't,' Joseph said.

But Yolanda nodded. 'Yes, they do. Elephants need to be near water because they need to bathe and drink a lot.'

'How many children would you need if you had an elephant on one side of the scale and children on the other and you wanted it to balance?'

'It'd be one huge scale.'

'Indeed it would. One average Asian adult elephant weighs about eight hundred and sixty stone. If all the children, thirty of you, and teachers at this school stood on the scale they wouldn't weigh as much as an elephant does.'

'Wow – they're so heavy.'

AJ hoped their elephant never sat on him because he'd be squashed as flat as a pancake.

'Did you know that men have used elephants in war since pre-Roman times?'

'Why don't they go to war now?' Simon asked.

'They could trample the Germans,' said Daisy. 'And then my dad could come home.'

'Not much room for an elephant in a trench,' Joseph said. 'My dad says there's not enough room to swing a cat in there.'

AJ thought swinging a cat, whether there was a lot of room or not, was a very bad idea.

'Who can tell me how long elephants live?' Mr Soames asked.

AJ and Yolanda looked at each other. Their dad hadn't mentioned that.

'Ten years?' Daisy asked.

Mr Soames shook his head. 'Much longer.'

'Thirty years,' said Joseph. That seemed like a very long time.

But Mr Soames shook his head again. 'Much longer than thirty years.'

'Sixty years?' said Yolanda.

'Longer still,' said Mr Soames. 'Elephants can live for seventy years or so.'

'As long as people,' AJ said.

'Yes, and their babies *are* a lot like human babies too. They can't eat solid food when they're born. Elephants need their mother's milk for at least the first three years of their lives. In lots of ways a two-year-old elephant is very much like a two-year-old child. Full of mischief, but still needing its mum to survive. And instead of sucking its thumb it sucks its trunk.'

For lunch the children had sausages in batter with potatoes and thick gravy.

'Mmm . . . toad-in-the-hole,' AJ said. It was his favourite.

Yolanda pushed some of hers on to her friend Daisy's plate when Mr Soames wasn't looking, although they weren't supposed to swap food.

But Daisy was always hungry and so was her brother Simon.

She gave AJ, who was sitting next to Simon, a pointed look.

AJ looked down at his plate and pushed it away.

'Too much for me,' he said, as Simon quickly scraped the rest of AJ's food on to his own plate.

As soon as school was finally over for the day, Yolanda and AJ jumped off the hard wooden school benches and ran all the way home. In a few hours they'd have a real-life elephant at the farm, sleeping in their barn.

Chapter 3

Harvey rested his grey-whiskered muzzle on Albert's knee, almost as if he sensed his friend's sadness, and Albert stroked his furry head. Albert had found Harvey soaking wet in a hedgerow when he was just a small puppy. It had been Albert's fifth birthday and his dad had been taking him into town for a birthday treat.

'Hello, little puppy,' he'd said, looking at the tiny dog that peeped up at him from amongst the leaves.

'Can I keep him?' Albert had asked his dad. 'For my birthday?'

'Hmm, we've got our hands full already . . . But I suppose he could be a good addition to the act,' Albert's dad had said, 'and he does seem like a friendly little chap.'

Albert had picked the puppy up and laughed as it reached up and licked his face.

'I'll call him Harvey,' he'd said, and Harvey had wagged his little puppy tail.

The two of them had grown up together and hadn't been apart since that day. He wished he could take the dog with him. He was sure Harvey would have made a good rat-catching dog – ratters were wanted out on the Western Front. Soldiers were even being paid to take them with them because they needed all the help they could get to keep down the rat infestation. But Albert was going to fight in the Middle East, and ratter dogs weren't wanted over there.

Albert sighed as he stood up to take off his costume and put on his new, uncomfortable army uniform instead. He patted Shanti's side as Tara cheekily put her trunk to his pocket to see if there was another apple there. Shanti and Tara were always peckish after a show and Albert made sure he had their food all ready for them.

Today it was mostly cabbages, but the elephants didn't seem to mind too much and ate them all up.

'You'll have lots of tasty farm food once you get to your new home,' Albert told them.

Harvey didn't eat cabbage even when he was very hungry and Albert had spent the last of his money on buying him a bone.

'Here you are,' he said as Harvey gently took it from him, tail wagging.

Albert smiled as he watched Harvey lying on the ground and gnawing on the bone enthusiastically. Money well spent.

Cabbages all eaten, Albert was confronted by Tara's inquisitive trunk. She often checked his nose with her trunk as if she couldn't work out where his was.

'Hey,' he said as she tugged at his face.

Fortunately Shanti never tried to do the same. A baby elephant pulling your nose was bad enough, but he dreaded to think what a full-grown elephant could do.

Tara made her laughing *squee* noise.

'Tara the terrible, that's what you should be called!' Albert told her affectionately. 'Tara the terrible!'

Tara nuzzled her face into his, not caring one little bit.

Albert swallowed hard. He was going to miss the baby elephant so much. His last day with Harvey, Shanti and Tara had sped past much too quickly.

But what was done was done, and he had to do his duty. His country needed him.

'What about the elephants?' Albert had said, when the ringmaster had urged him to enlist as they passed through Lancaster at the end of August. 'I can't just leave them.'

'Don't you worry about them, they can help on the home front,' the ringmaster had said.

'They can?' Albert asked, as the ringmaster pushed him inside the recruiting office. Tara was far too young to do any heavy work. She was still only a baby, a toddler really. 'What are they going to do?'

'I've found them a new home on a farm. Shanti will be doing a bit of forest log transporting and other farm work,' the ringmaster told him. 'Tara will be mostly watching her mum. They'll get plenty of fresh air and good food to eat. Probably have a better life than in the circus.'

Albert liked the idea of the elephants being outside more rather than stuck in the circus tent. But he was still worried about them.

'Where are they being sent to?'

'Lake District.'

'Whereabouts?'

'Stony Oakhill.'

Albert had never even heard of the place.

'Why didn't you mention it before?'

The ringmaster looked a bit sheepish.

'I was going to tell you when we got back to the site. Only just heard about it myself. All got to do our part for the war effort haven't we? If the army can requisition horses they can requisition elephants too – and camels.'

The ringmaster put his arm round Albert's shoulders as they stopped in front of the recruiting desk.

'You want the best for your elephants, don't you? You know this will be best for them.'

'We're looking for men who know about camels for the Camel Corps,' the recruiter said.

'Well, this is your man,' the ringmaster told him, pushing Albert forward. 'Been in the circus his whole life and not much he doesn't know about the beast.'

Albert thought this was a bit of an exaggeration. He'd only been on a camel a few times.

'How old are you, lad?' the recruiter asked Albert.

'Fif–' Albert started to say.

'Nineteen,' the ringmaster interrupted. 'I can vouch for that.'

'Where is the camel battalion based?' Albert asked the recruiter.

'Egypt,' he was told. 'Sign here.' The recruiter held out a pen to him.

And Albert almost took it.

'But what about Harvey?' he said to the ringmaster. 'What'll happen to him?'

'He'll be coming with me,' the ringmaster said. 'You know I've always had a soft spot for the dog.' He took the pen from the recruiter and gave it to Albert and Albert signed the form.

'Your dad would be proud of you,' the ringmaster told him.

Now, three weeks later, it was time to leave.

'Ready?' the ringmaster asked, pulling back the tent flap and startling Albert. 'Don't want to miss that train.'

Albert swallowed hard, fighting back the urge to cry out that he didn't want to go. It had all been a terrible mistake. He should never have let the ringmaster persuade him to enlist. He shouldn't have listened when he'd told him that it was the right thing to do and his father would have been proud of him. 'You're sure the animals –'

'They will be fine,' the ringmaster said. 'The elephants will be helping out on the home front and Harvey will be with me.' He went to stroke Harvey, but the dog picked up his now meatless bone and headed over to Shanti to carry on eating it underneath her. The ringmaster sniffed. 'Not like there's going to be a circus any more for them to be part of anyway. We'll all have gone our separate ways before the week's out.'

Albert nodded but couldn't trust himself to speak.

'I'll give you a minute to say your goodbyes,' the ringmaster told him. 'But don't take too long.'

Harvey came out from underneath Shanti as soon as the ringmaster had gone and Albert hugged him to him.

'You be a good dog now, you hear?' he said.

Harvey sat still and tilted his head to one side and then slowly put out a front paw to him which Albert translated as more strokes please. Once he'd patted him some more Albert took the note he'd written to the elephants' new owner over to Shanti.

'Head, Shanti,' he said, and when the elephant lowered her head he put the note inside the pocket behind the star on her headdress. Albert thought it might help if their new owner continued to use the commands the elephants were already used to, so he'd written them all down.

'Goodbye, sweet Shanti,' Albert said, as Tara plonked her trunk on top of his head and ruffled his hair again. 'Goodbye, little Tara the terrible,' Albert laughed as he turned and hugged the baby elephant. 'Goodbye, Harvey,' he said, as the dog whined and put out his paw again.

'Time to go!' the ringmaster shouted. 'It's almost five o'clock.'

'Coming,' said Albert, picking up his brown cardboard suitcase.

Harvey got up to go with him.

'No, Harvey, you wait here,' Albert said.

Harvey whined again. He didn't want to wait.

'Sit,' said Albert.

Harvey sat.

'Now stay,' Albert said, and he swallowed hard and left the tent to join the ringmaster.

'No time to lose,' the ringmaster said, as they headed briskly for Whitehaven railway station.

'I thought I saw Carl from Cullen's Circus in the audience this afternoon,' Albert told the ringmaster, as they walked.

'Did you?' the ringmaster frowned. 'Doesn't seem very likely. Are you absolutely sure?'

And now Albert wasn't quite so sure. 'I . . . I think so.'

Carl's cruel treatment of Shanti was the reason Albert's dad had made them leave the much larger and more successful Cullen's Circus for the smaller Lewis Brothers' one. His dad said he wished they could take all of the elephants away from there. But they weren't rich enough to do so and had used just about all their savings buying Shanti. Of course they hadn't known she was newly pregnant when they'd bought her and an elephant's pregnancy lasts almost two years so Tara hadn't come along for a long time and was quite a surprise when she did.

But the ringmaster had been delighted. 'Two elephants for the price of one! You should be celebrating,' he said to Albert's father.

Carl and his boss were reported to have been furious when they found out Shanti had given birth to a healthy calf.

'Hardly time to draw a breath let alone look out at the audience whilst you're doing your act, surely,' the ringmaster continued, interrupting Albert's thoughts. 'Especially keeping that young Tara in check.'

'And you're sure the new owner is used to elephants?' Albert asked again.

'Yes, yes – we've been through this. Don't you worry, it's all sorted out,' the ringmaster said, as they headed briskly into the station and out on to the platform where Albert's train was already waiting.

But Albert did worry. 'Tara can be a bit of a handful,' he said.

'Everyone has their moments,' the ringmaster told him.

'What are you going to do yourself now that the circus has disbanded?' Albert asked the ringmaster. He'd been so busy thinking about himself that he hadn't given a thought to the older man, now that his livelihood had gone.

'Oh, I'll think of something –'

The ringmaster was interrupted by a loud bark that Albert would have recognized anywhere.

His heart leapt as he turned round to find Harvey bounding towards him.

'I told you to wait, Harvey,' Albert said, but he was smiling and Harvey knew he was pleased to see him.

'Dozy dog,' the ringmaster muttered as Albert crouched down and Harvey ran over to him and licked his face. Albert laughed and buried his face in Harvey's fur so the ringmaster wouldn't see his tears.

'You're sure you don't mind looking after him while I'm away?' Albert said.

The ringmaster shook his head. 'Not at all.' He opened the carriage door. 'In you get now.'

Harvey whined and tried to follow Albert on to the train, but the ringmaster's boot pushed him roughly back.

A moment later the train whistled and started to move off with a whoosh of steam.

Harvey barked again and again. Where was Albert going without him? He didn't want to be left behind. He looked up at the train with Albert on it and he started to whine as the train slowly moved away. The next moment Harvey was running down the platform after the train, barking as he swerved in between the people on the platform. He wanted to be with Albert wherever he went, whatever he was doing.

Albert saw Harvey and pushed down the window.

'Go back, Harvey!' he shouted. 'Please, please go back.'

There was nothing he would have liked more than to have Harvey with him, but the dog wouldn't like the heat of the desert, even if the army allowed him to keep him. He was better off staying here and being cared for by the ringmaster.

The platform came to an end but Harvey still ran on, desperately following the train. He ran and ran until he couldn't run any more and could only watch as the train sped on ever further into the distance taking Albert away from him.

Harvey threw back his head and howled his despair up into the sky.

Then he lay down with his head in his paws and waited for the metal beast that had taken his Albert away from him to return. But the train didn't come back.

'Come on you,' growled the ringmaster, as he looped a rope round Harvey's neck and pulled him up.

'You're coming with me.'

Chapter 4

Tara had never met the red-faced man with the broken nose before and so she didn't know that she was supposed to be frightened of him when he came into the elephant tent.

But Shanti remembered Carl from the time she'd spent at Cullen's Circus and she trembled with fear and moved as far away from him as she could get, which wasn't very far as the tent was small.

Unaware, Tara trotted over to Carl and opened her mouth wide hoping for a treat. But when Shanti saw what she was doing she hurried over and blocked her daughter from the man.

Carl looked into Shanti's big eyes. 'Remember me, do you? They say an elephant never forgets.'

He lifted up a long stick with a straight sharp point like a spear on one end and beside it a curved point like a hook. Elephant's skin looked thick but Carl knew that it was very sensitive and in some places paper thin and incredibly tender. Carl knew where all those places were and how to use the elephant goad to inflict the most pain. Elephants soon learnt to obey his every command.

'Remember this?' he said.

'Right,' said the ringmaster, coming into the tent. 'The boy's gone and the little elephant is yours now.'

'Should have always been mine,' Carl said, pointing the elephant goad at Tara. 'The father's one of our bulls so the daughter belongs to Cullen's.'

The ringmaster had heard this a hundred times before. 'Well she's yours now, as I promised she would be in return for a job at Cullen's. Let's get her mother on to the train.' He hadn't told Albert about the two hundred pounds he'd been paid for Shanti and he didn't tell Carl either. 'We've wasted enough time already today.'

But Shanti didn't want to go anywhere without her daughter.

Harvey was tied up outside the ringmaster's caravan when he heard the terrible distressed sounds coming from the elephant tent, and he wrenched himself free.

The ringmaster and Carl were trying to force Shanti out of the tent having tied up Tara to a stake in the ground, to prevent her from following her mother. Carl pushed the sharp spike of the elephant goad at Shanti into the sensitive spots on her skin and her soft ears. Shanti cried out in pain, but refused to leave Tara, however much they struck her.

Harvey barked and ran towards the ringmaster and Carl who were hurting his friend. He growled, but they didn't stop. As Carl went to strike Shanti again Harvey clamped on to his brown trouser leg with his sharp teeth.

'Ger-roff!' Carl tried to shake Harvey away. 'That mutt will need to learn some discipline, too if he's coming with you,' he snarled at the ringmaster.

But Harvey didn't let go, pulling harder on Carl's trouser leg until Carl turned and lashed out at him with the elephant goad. Harvey yelped in pain. The hook was as sharp as a knife and it tore through the fur on his leg to his skin and drew blood. Harvey whined and slowly backed away.

'That'll show him who's boss,' Carl said, as they turned their attention back to Shanti.

The ringmaster took the opportunity to grab Harvey by the scruff of his neck.

'You're supposed to be tied up,' he said roughly, pulling Harvey back. Both men were out of breath from all the effort.

'They'd never dare to behave like this if they were at Cullen's Circus,' Carl said.

The ringmaster was getting a bit tired of hearing about how much better Cullen's was. He looked down at Harvey, whom he now tied firmly to a tent pole, licking his leg wound.

'Right, bring the baby elephant – it's the only way we'll get her mother on the train,' the ringmaster said. 'That's the thing about elephants,' he continued, mopping the sweat from his brow with his handkerchief. 'Well, all animals except humans, really.'

Carl raised an eyebrow. 'What's that then?'

'They don't lie so they're easy to trick.'

The ringmaster released the rope holding Tara to the ground stake and the little elephant ran to her mother, squealing in distress. Shanti wrapped her trunk round her and made soothing sounds to her frightened daughter. She looked over at Harvey, who jumped up and pulled against the tent peg, leg wound forgotten.

'Right, let's get going,' the ringmaster said, taking hold of the rope round Tara's neck. 'He's not going anywhere,' he added with a nod at Harvey. Harvey let out a low growl.

Shanti looked over at Harvey and reached out to him with her trunk. But before she could touch him Carl prodded her with the horrible goad, while the ringmaster pulled Tara out of the tent. Shanti's attention quickly turned to her daughter and she followed them.

'Just need a little bit of guile,' the ringmaster said smugly as he led Tara along the road towards the freight siding. There was no way an elephant, or a dog, or even most humans were getting the better of him.

It was already almost six o'clock, but it was still light when they got to the station. They got some strange looks from the passengers as the stationmaster directed them to the goods-train siding far away from the passenger platforms to wait for the train that would transport Shanti.

'No special elephant carriage?' Carl said, when the train finally pulled in and the ringmaster headed towards a livestock carriage used for horses.

'Too expensive,' Jedediah told him.

'But what if the elephant breaks out?'

'She won't – and anyway if she gets out of a moving train and injures herself, well, that won't be our fault, will it? We sent her off in a calm, placid condition. Can't help it if something spooks her on the journey, can we?'

He led Tara up the ramp into the horse carriage and Shanti quickly followed her, just as the ringmaster had hoped.

There wasn't much room inside but Shanti still tried to protect her daughter by getting in between Tara and Carl. The horse carriage had no windows and was hot from being shut up all day. It smelt musty and Shanti trembled as she lay her trunk along her terrified daughter's back. Both elephants' eyes were wide with fear and pain.

'Chain Shanti up then,' said the ringmaster and Carl set to work, winding the strong chains back and forth round Shanti's legs, her neck and her trunk and back.

'Got enough chains to hold four elephants here,' Carl said. 'No way this one's going anywhere.'

'Good,' said the ringmaster. 'All secure? Now it's time for you to come with us,' he said, turning his attention to Tara who was standing as close to her mother as she could and touching her with her trunk. He gave the baby elephant a sharp prod with the elephant goad to force her out of the carriage.

Tara gave a squeal of surprise and pain. She'd never been struck before. Shanti bellowed and pulled against the chains, but they held fast. Carl pulled at the rope round Tara's neck with one hand and grabbed one of her ears with the other.

'Come on!'

The ringmaster struck and pushed the little elephant from behind forcing her away from her mother.

Shanti bellowed in desperation and despair as she twisted and turned, but the chains didn't give way as they tore into her flesh. The door slammed shut and she was left in darkness as Tara was dragged away, screaming and crying.

Shanti roared and roared and got herself more and more tangled up until she was kneeling rather than standing, but she couldn't break free of her chains in the hot, airless carriage.

The ringmaster gave the station crew and the conductor some money for their inconvenience.

'The new owner'll need this,' Carl said, handing over the elephant goad to the conductor.

'Won't you need it?' the ringmaster asked, surprised at Carl's unusual generosity.

'Got plenty more back at Cullen's,' Carl told him. 'And a stick'll be enough to keep the little one in line.'

'No point us heading off till the morning now is there?' the ringmaster asked Carl as they forced Tara along the street back to the circus. 'We'll have some supper and a bottle or two back the caravan once we've sorted the little elephant out.'

Carl thought that was a very good idea. Herding elephants was hungry and thirsty work.

In the darkness of the horse carriage, with the windows boarded up, Shanti finally stopped roaring and trying to break free from the chains that bound her. Tara had gone.

Tears fell from the mother elephant's eyes as the whistle blew and the train left the station.

Chapter 5

At last, Yolanda heard the sound of their dad's study door opening and the squeak of his wheelchair wheels.

'You two ready?' Mr Jones called out. 'Ajaz?'

Only his dad ever called him that. Everyone else always called him AJ.

'Yes, Dad,' AJ shouted.

'At last,' Yolanda said, as the two of them scrambled off the sofa.

AJ pushed his dad's squeaky-wheeled wheelchair as the three of them headed to Stony Oakhill railway station, ten minutes' walk away. Yolanda walked behind pushing a wheelbarrow full of food for the elephant.

'Your wheels need oiling, Dad,' she said.

'I know. I'm reminding myself of a giant-sized mouse,' he smiled.

'Elephants don't eat people, do they?' AJ asked him. He'd been worrying about an elephant biting him quite a lot ever since he'd learnt that they were going to have one living with them. Last night he'd had a nasty dream about becoming an elephant's supper. He had to ask his dad now. It would be too late by the time the elephant arrived. He had to know.

'Of course not,' Yolanda said, her eyes opening wide. 'Why on earth would you think that?'

AJ didn't seem to have listened to anything Mr Soames had tried to teach them at school today.

'Elephants only eat plant foods,' their dad said, and AJ sighed with relief. That was all right then.

'They're frightened of tiny mice aren't they, Dad?' Yolanda said.

But their dad wasn't quite sure if they were frightened of them or not. 'It could be a myth,' he said. 'We'll have to see.'

'It'll probably be terrified of all the mice in the barn then,' AJ said, and then he gulped as he found he had a whole new problem to worry about. What if the elephant got frightened and stampeded and what if . . . what if . . . it was so terrible he couldn't say it out loud . . . what if *he* got in its way by mistake? Being run over by an elephant would be a *lot* worse than being bitten by one.

'Here we are,' his dad said, and they turned into the station.

'We've come to pick up Shanti,' AJ told the stationmaster.

'Our elephant,' said Yolanda.

'Have you indeed?' the stationmaster said, and he pointed along the platform. 'You'll find it in a carriage in the sidings. Just follow the noise.'

As they got closer they could hear a deep mournful rumbling noise coming from a horse carriage without windows. Some of the station workers were standing outside it and they pulled open the door as they arrived.

Yolanda and AJ stared at the elephant bundled up like a parcel with chains. Her eyes stared at them desperately.

Yolanda felt sick. Why was the elephant being treated like this?

'Why's she chained up like that?' AJ asked.

The elephant couldn't even move her head.

'Needs to be,' one of the station men said.

'Only way,' said another.

'All those chains wouldn't be strong enough to hold a crazed elephant,' the first man said.

'Elephants can be very dangerous,' said the second.

'Unchain her,' Mr Jones said.

The station crew didn't look like they thought this was a very good idea.

'Are you sure that's wise, sir?' one of them asked.

'Yes,' AJ and Yolanda's dad said.

'Your funeral,' the man sighed, hoping it wouldn't be his funeral too.

Two of them released the chains that had been wound like a spider's web around Shanti's legs and trunk to hobble her. She had raw cuts on her skin where she'd pulled against them, but hadn't been able to break free. The elephant rocked from side to side as the mournful sounds continued.

'Is there a storm coming?' AJ asked.

One of the station men looked up at the sky. It was perfectly clear.

'It's coming from Shanti.' Yolanda said. She too sensed the low throbbing AJ had felt, although it was so low she couldn't hear it. 'It makes me feel weird.'

'It makes me feel like I do when there's thunder in the air,' said AJ.

The station man shrugged.

'I think I know what it is,' said Mr Jones. 'It's the elephant call. When I was in Ceylon, people spoke of the special song that only elephants can hear. It's too low for most humans to detect, although some people, like you, may feel it as a throbbing sensation like when there's a very deep note on the organ in church.'

AJ nodded.

'The elephant's call can travel for miles and other elephants can hear it. I expect Shanti's calling out because she's been so distressed shut up in that carriage,' Mr Jones said. 'Elephants are able to meet up in the same exact spot at the same time when they've been miles apart, thanks to that song.'

'I'd be crying out if I was shut in there too,' AJ said. 'Poor Shanti must have been so frightened.'

'It's stopped now,' Yolanda said. She looked at the elephant and had never felt so sorry for a creature in her life.

'You'll be needing this,' another of the station men said, picking up a stick with a sharp hook at the end of it. 'Circus folk told us it'd get the brute to do what you needed it to do.'

Shanti shied away from the sight of the elephant goad.

'We will most certainly not be needing that,' Mr Jones said firmly.

Once the chains were off Shanti started to move and the station men quickly jumped out of the horse carriage.

'Don't want to get stepped on by an elephant,' one of them told AJ.

AJ couldn't agree more. The elephant was absolutely huge. Bigger than the steam engine Annie and the other the Land Army girls used before it was taken away. Twice as tall as him, and ten of him could stand side by side and still only just be as long as her.

'Elephants' feet are very sensitive,' his dad told him. 'So that probably wouldn't happen.'

AJ breathed a sigh of relief.

'Their footpads are filled with a special sort of oil and really pretty amazing,' Mr Jones continued. 'They can pick up tiny vibrations in the ground as elephants call to each other. Like whales do.'

They put a ramp up by the horse carriage door, but Shanti didn't come down it. She just stood at the door looking out at them. Then she raised her trunk and sniffed the air. There was not even the faintest scent of Tara in any direction.

Yolanda looked up at the huge beast.

'She's been crying,' she said, staring at the half-dried tears on Shanti's face.

'She's very sad,' AJ said.

'All elephants look a little sad,' his dad told him. 'It's the way their faces are.'

But AJ didn't believe him. He knew sadness when he saw it.

'Here, Shanti,' Yolanda called to the elephant, holding out a carrot from the wheelbarrow to her.

Shanti came down the ramp a little way, stretched out her trunk, took the carrot from Yolanda and ate it. Then she came down the ramp a little further, plucked a cabbage from the pile of vegetables in the wheelbarrow and ate that too.

'That's it, Shanti,' Mr Jones said. 'Move back with the wheelbarrow,' he told Yolanda. 'Brisk march back to the farm now. Quick.'

Shanti followed the wheelbarrow, helping herself to tasty carrots and apples, cabbages and maize while Yolanda kept the wheelbarrow moving as fast as she could because even when

Shanti was walking slowly she was still going quickly.

'It's like the donkey and the carrot on the stick story,' AJ said as he pushed his dad's wheelchair behind Shanti and Yolanda.

The news that the elephant had finally arrived at the station, and was on its way to Mr Jones's farm, had spread through Stony Oakhill like wildfire. Villagers came out of their cottages to see Shanti. Some of them brought more food for the elephant.

'Here, elephant, here,' a lady said, holding out half a loaf of stale bread.

Shanti whisked the bread away from her with her trunk and swallowed it in a single gulp.

Others weren't so brave and rolled cabbages to the elephant instead. Shanti picked them up in her trunk, took them to her mouth and swallowed them down.

'Wheelbarrow's almost empty and we're not home yet,' Yolanda said.

Shanti was determined to finish off every last small plum and potato from the very bottom of the barrow and she kept on helping herself all the way through the village until they reached Forest View Farm and the barn that was to be her new home.

'Home at last,' said Yolanda and not a moment too soon. The wheelbarrow was now completely empty.

The children pulled open the barn door. The barn had been filled with sweet-smelling hay and straw and although they thought Shanti should have been full she ate some of that too.

AJ was worried again.

'Should we tie her up?' he asked, looking round for anything they could use. They'd left the chains she'd been shackled with back at the station, along with the elephant goad.

'Why?' his dad asked him.

'In case she runs away.'

'If an elephant truly wanted to run away there'd be nothing we could do to stop it,' his dad said.

'Oh,' said AJ, now worrying that the elephant would run away.

'Although it might be good if we put a cow bell round her neck so people are warned when she's heading their way, that's what we did in Ceylon.'

'Should we take her beautiful headdress off?' Yolanda asked.

But her dad shook his head. 'I think it's best if we leave her be, let her adjust to her new home for tonight. There's potatoes and carrots over in the corner and more hay up in the hay loft which she can reach with her trunk.'

'She can't still be hungry after all the food she's had!' AJ grinned.

'Elephants eat up to three hundred pounds of vegetation a day,' Mr Jones said. 'And fifty gallons of water. There's a fresh barrel of water by the door if she's thirsty and we need to make sure it keeps being refilled. But why don't we give her some space and let her rest now. It's time you two had your supper and got some rest too.'

'I'll get it ready,' said Yolanda.

'Oh no, Dad. I'm not hungry at all,' AJ said, although he was really. He just didn't want to leave Shanti yet.

'You'll have plenty of time to be with her tomorrow. Come on now.'

'Night, Shanti,' said AJ, waving to her as he left.

'Sleep well,' said Yolanda, and she touched her trunk before following the others out of the barn, pulling the door to behind her.

Yolanda and AJ were in bed when Shanti's mournful bellowing began.

'Maybe having an elephant living with us isn't going to be such a good idea,' Yolanda said, creeping into AJ's room. 'I didn't know elephants could be so noisy.'

'I told you she was sad,' said AJ, sitting up. He knew the elephant was unhappy, whatever their dad said.

When it was very late and dark and the farm was quiet, Shanti pushed open the barn door and went outside. She'd never been apart from Tara before and missing her was so painful she couldn't bear it.

She stood on the farm path and called to Tara using the elephants' special deep call that was too low for people to hear. Her sensitive feet and ears were attuned for the slightest familiar vibration. There was no reply, but she didn't stop. She carried on calling to her daughter throughout the night.

Finally, just before dawn, she returned to the barn, went inside, lay down on the straw and fell asleep.

Chapter 6

By the time Carl and the ringmaster returned from the station, Harvey had finally managed to bite his way through the string that tied him to the tent peg and had gone – but not far.

He watched from the bushes as the men dragged the little elephant back into the tent.

'Dog's gone,' Carl said.

'Good riddance to it,' said Jedediah. He'd never wanted the old dog anyway.

Harvey waited until the ringmaster and Carl had left the tent and then he crept back to it.

Tara was tied with so many ropes that she couldn't even stand up. The ropes had cut into her tender skin, but that wasn't why she was sobbing. She was crying for her mum. They weren't ever supposed to be apart, but now Shanti was gone.

Harvey crawled over to her and whined as Carl and the ringmaster clinked glasses and celebrated in the caravan next door.

Tara put her trunk out to him and he lay close to her. But nothing he could do could stop her from trembling.

Harvey didn't know where Shanti was. But he did know how to bite through a rope and once he'd bitten through the first one he was able to help Tara unwind herself and soon the baby elephant was free.

The tent flap wasn't secured and Harvey had opened it many times before. He looked up at Tara who had her trunk over his back. If she made her distinctive trumpet sound now their escape attempt would be discovered. Luckily the little elephant kept quiet and the sensitive soft padding on the bottom of her feet made her footfall as soundless as Harvey's as the two of them slipped out of the tent and headed off into the night.

Tara knew where they needed to go: back the way the men had taken her – back to where they'd left her mum – and she broke into a run with Harvey running along behind her.

Before tonight Harvey had never been tempted to stray far from the circus where Albert and the two elephants that were his family were. But now he knew that he and Tara had to get away. The scent of Shanti was still strong as he and Tara headed back to the railway siding. But Shanti was no longer there.

Tara had never been more than a few feet away from her mum in her life before today. Every night since she'd been born they'd slept with their trunks curled round each other. She called and called to her with the low rumbling elephant call, but her mum didn't reply. Her head sank low as she stretched her trunk gently across Harvey's back for comfort. The dog walked close to her so that she could feel his comforting warmth beside her. The little elephant hadn't eaten anything since her mother had gone and her belly rumbled with hunger. Normally she had milk every few hours. She was thirsty too. There'd been no water since Albert had left.

But they didn't stop. The blackout that had been imposed across the country because of the fear of Zeppelins meant the two animals were able to pass out of the town of Whitehaven and into the countryside following the railway track unseen. Once there it didn't matter if Tara made a sound. But she was too miserable to make her usual happy squeeing noise and called desperately into the air for her mum over and over instead, but Shanti never replied and the scent of her was gone now. They headed on towards the coast and away from the circus that was no longer their home.

Harvey and Tara hadn't been gone for more than an hour when Carl decided to check on the little elephant.

'She should have stopped squealing for her mother by now,' he said, as he staggered out of the ringmaster's caravan. The night was beautiful and clear. Warm too.

He pulled back the elephant tent flap and went inside. It was darker inside the tent than out, but he'd still expected to see a grey baby-elephant-shaped lump on the floor. He headed over to where he'd left Tara tied up as tight as could be. It didn't make sense. He rubbed at his eyes. Where was she? He looked behind him and around the edges of the tent.

He stumbled over something and picked it up. It was one of the ropes he'd used to tie Tara up. More of the rope lay scattered about. How on earth had the baby elephant managed to free herself?

The ringmaster came in a few moments later with a lantern. Now they could both clearly see that Tara definitely wasn't there. They stared at the ropes on the floor.

'Someone must have helped her,' Carl said. He'd tied those ropes himself. There was no way they could have just loosened themselves.

'It wasn't a someone. It was a *something*. Those ropes haven't been untied or cut, they've been chewed through.'

'Chewed?' Carl said.

'Yes, and I know who by,' Jedediah said. 'That dog . . .'

Carl sat down on a hay bale.

'She might not have got far yet,' Jedediah said. 'We could follow her.'

But Carl just shook his head, a weird look on his face. 'She could've got quite a way away by now and we don't know in which direction she's gone. Best to let nature take its course.'

'What do you mean?' Jedediah asked, his blood running cold.

'Baby elephants are a lot like baby humans. She's only what – two?' Carl said.

Jedediah nodded. 'Just turned two.'

'An elephant that young won't survive without its mother for long.'

'But we can't just let her starve!' Jedediah said, feeling dazed and a bit sick at what he was hearing. He'd just wanted some extra cash when he'd agreed to sell Shanti. But he hadn't thought for a moment that her daughter would have to die because of it. The deal was he'd let Carl have Tara in exchange for a job at Cullen's Circus. But now he wished he'd never made the dreadful deal. He'd been a fool.

'Better get some sleep before we head over to Cullen's,' Carl said. 'Don't want those elephants forgetting who's in charge.'

'I won't be coming with you to Cullen's in the morning after all,' Jedediah said slowly. His mind made up.

'Suit yourself,' Carl said. 'Makes no difference to me.'

As they trudged on into the early hours of the morning Tara's walk became slower and slower. It had been a terrifying and exhausting day for the young elephant and she needed time and sleep to process all that had happened, as well as to grieve for the loss of her mum.

Harvey was exhausted too and his leg hurt from where it had been cut.

When Tara staggered and then lay down in the road, all Harvey wanted was to lie down too, but he headed towards the safety of some nearby bushes where they wouldn't be so easily seen. He whined at the little elephant and Tara, who more than anything didn't want to be left alone, crawled to her feet, stumbled her way over to him, lay down in the bushes and fell instantly asleep with a little sigh.

Harvey watched her sleeping as he listened to the night-sounds of the wild animals in the woods around them before his eyelids grew heavy and he slept too.

Chapter 7

AJ and Yolanda, who'd fallen asleep to the sound of Shanti's bellowing, were woken the next morning by the sound of the cockerel crowing.

'We've got an elephant,' said AJ.

'A real-life elephant,' said Yolanda.

And they ran down the stairs and out of the front door to go and see her. But when they got to the barn, Shanti wasn't there.

'Where is she?' Yolanda asked.

'She must have run away,' said AJ. But he didn't want her to have done. Not one bit.

'Her water's all gone,' Yolanda said.

'And so's her food,' said AJ.

They both had the same idea at the same time.

'Maybe she's gone to find some more!'

Just then, they heard the sound of ducks angrily quacking and geese squawking and hurried out of the barn and along the farm track towards the pond.

Shanti had drunk all of the water in the barrel in the barn so she decided to go outside to find some more. The ginger-and-white farm cat, Tiger, looked round from the mouse he was stalking, gave a yowl and jumped up on to the stone wall round the herb garden when he saw her. But he didn't hiss as he would usually have done – she was much too big to risk doing that.

Shanti went on down the farm path, past the stall that had once belonged to Noodles the donkey, and past the stables that had been the homes of Buttercup and Bluebell before they'd been requisitioned.

At the end of the stables there was a barrel of rainwater and Shanti took a long, long drink.

The few cows that the farm had were in the small pasture to the left, and on the rocky grassland and hills above were the sheep. Shanti had half turned to go and investigate the sheep and cows, when she spotted the pond.

Usually, Albert gave her and Tara a bath in the morning. And now it was morning and Albert wasn't there so Shanti decided to give herself a bath.

The geese came rushing at her, honking, but with a squawk and a rustling of feathers quickly made way for her to pass as she strolled on. Shanti knew where she wanted to be and she wasn't going to be distracted by squawking birds, be they geese or the ducks that were already on the pond.

The banks were very muddy and it wasn't easy for a big elephant to get into the pond as the sides were slippery. Shanti normally preferred a firmer footing, but she managed. And once she had got into the water she found it wasn't very deep, at least not for an elephant. She sat down in the middle of the pond with the ducks watching from the banks, dipped her trunk under the surface to suck up some water and then squirted it, along with some mud, over her back.

'Shanti!' AJ called, as he and Yolanda came running.

The big elephant looked over at him and raised her trunk in greeting, before scooping up more squelchy mud from the bottom of the pond and depositing it on her head.

'Her beautiful headdress will be ruined,' cried Yolanda.

'I don't think Shanti cares much about beautiful headdresses,' said AJ. And he laughed as he looked at Shanti's muddy new look.

'She's so beautiful,' Yolanda said. 'I never realized quite how beautiful elephants are before we had Shanti come to live with us.'

'What if she won't come out?' said AJ. He didn't envy anyone who had to try and persuade an elephant to do something it didn't want to do.

'She'll come out in her own time,' their father said, rolling along the path to join them. 'We'll just have to wait for her.'

They didn't have to wait long. Shanti gave a trumpet and came out of the pond a few moments later. She wasn't used to duck ponds and bathing herself – Albert had always done it for her.

Yolanda couldn't bear to see the headdress ruined. It had almost fallen off Shanti's muddy wet head and now it dropped on the ground. Yolanda picked it up.

'I think I can repair it,' she said. 'Or at least give it a wash.'

'What's that,' AJ asked, pointing to the bit of white paper sticking out from the star.

Yolanda pulled it out.

'It looks like a letter, but it's got wet and some of the letters have run. I can't read it properly.'

The two children and their father pored over the paper while Shanti stood watching them.

'Can you make any of it out?'

'Just a name – "Tara".'

'Who's Tara?'

When she heard her daughter's name. Shanti gave a bellowing trumpet that made them all jump.

'Do you think it's her friend? They might have had lots of elephants at the circus she came from, or at least two or three.'

'Which circus did she come from?'

'Lewis Brothers'.'

'Do elephants have friends?'

'I don't see why not.'

Mr Jones looked down at the paper and tried to decipher more of it but it was impossible.

'I hope it wasn't anything too urgent. I'm sure it can't be. Her headdress isn't the safest of places.'

'So what should we do?' Yolanda asked.

'I think the best thing to do is write to the ringmaster I bought Shanti from and ask him what the note said,' Mr Jones decided. 'You two go and get Shanti's food ready. I expect she's hungry.'

'I bet she's always hungry,' grinned AJ.

Shanti looked after the children as they ran off and made a soft sad sound.

'Don't worry they'll be back soon,' Mr Jones told the elephant. 'And they'll be bringing your breakfast.'

Chapter 8

It was just after dawn and the sky was streaked with pink when Tara was awoken by a bluebottle landing on her. She'd fallen asleep in a bush not far from the railway track alongside Harvey who was still sleeping. But now she was awake, her strong sense of smell picked up an interesting salty scent and with it, far off, but not too far away for an elephant to hear, was the whoosh of waves.

Harvey woke as soon as Tara stood up. He staggered to his feet and yelped at the pain from the injury he'd suffered the day before.

Nevertheless he trotted after the little elephant as she headed, almost at a trot now, towards the exciting smell.

A few hundred yards brought them to the long, sandy beach of St Bees.

Neither Tara nor Harvey had ever seen sand before, and the beach at St Bees stretched for miles. It felt different under her feet from the grass and stone Tara had been used to. Better somehow, softer and easier to kick up. She started to run along it with Harvey, still aching, hobbling after her – the sea wind whipping around them.

But suddenly, Tara stopped, so quickly that Harvey almost ran into the back of her. The little elephant raised her trunk to the pink sky and made a mournful sound totally unlike her usual laughing squee, but very like the sounds Harvey had heard the night before. It came from deep within her – an elephant cry to her mother, but Shanti did not reply.

A moment later Tara began running to the sea. She was thirsty and here was water, lots and lots of it. Harvey chased after her, barking at her to slow down, be careful, look where she was going. None of which the baby elephant listened to.

Her trunk went into the waves and she sucked up the water and then took it to her mouth and swallowed it all down. Harvey lapped at the wavy water too. It didn't taste quite right, but he was very thirsty so he kept on drinking it.

Then he was sick. Tara retched too and then was sick as well, right beside him on the sand.

But it didn't stop her from wanting to go into the wavy water. She paddled out as the sea washed over her feet and then over her knees, until finally she was forced to push her way through the water as it did its best to push her back.

Harvey didn't follow her in. He didn't like the water that had made him sick. He didn't like the way the waves came for him either, and he jumped back as they rushed towards him. He barked from the edge to tell Tara to come back, but she was having too much fun in the wavy water to listen to him.

Harvey barked even louder when she went out further still into the sea. He ran along the beach and back again whimpering as a wave went right over her head and she disappeared. But Tara wasn't fazed at all by it and the next second her feet could no longer feel the seabed beneath them and she instinctively started swimming through the water.

Harvey was frantic with fear for her as she went further and further out. He hobbled up and down, left to right, barking to her to come back. And finally she must have heard him because she turned and he was very relieved to see her swimming towards him, but only to worry him again by rolling on to her side in the shallower water and start using her trunk as a snorkel.

Further out to sea, in a small rowing boat, young Tom was with his grandfather helping him check the crab pots, as he usually did.

'At least the crabs aren't affected by the war,' his grandfather said. 'Plenty of crabs about still, but not plenty of anything else much.'

The old man sat staring into the sea lost in thought. 'It's gone on for far too long,' he said, half to himself. 'And what's it all for? Greed, that's what it's for, and millions of lads who don't even have a penn'orth of land to call their own have to lose their lives because someone else wants more of it.'

'Grandad . . .' Tom said.

He was looking shorewards at a grey rock that seemed to be moving in and out of the waves, and a dog barking at it. It looked almost as if the grey rock had an arm coming from it, although it was hard to see for absolute sure because of the sea spray and the brightness of the early morning sky.

But there was definitely something different about the shoreline today. He saw it again and stood up in the boat.

'Careful, lad,' his grandfather warned him.

'It looks like there's an elephant in the water,' Tom said. 'An elephant!'

His grandfather looked too, but his old eyes weren't as sharp as Tom's ten-year-old ones.

'What are you talking about?' he said.

And now Tom couldn't see it either. 'There was an elephant. No – yes – look, there it is again.'

They were still a long way out, and the tide was against them, but Tom started rowing towards the beach.

*

Harvey was hungry, and the saltwater had scratched his throat. He hadn't had to catch his own food for a very long time, but now his hunger brought his hunter instinct to the fore. When he saw the crab scuttling along the beach, he pounced on it, his jaws clamping round it. Harvey was an old dog, but there was nothing wrong with his teeth.

He finished it off as Tara finished playing in the waves and came back to the shore. She started kicking at the sand with her front foot to soften it and then used her trunk to scoop it up and throw it over her back. Her headdress was looking very much the worse for wear, but somehow it had managed to stay on her.

Harvey headed for some rock pools where food was even easier to find and chomped on an oyster and some razor clams.

Tara had been hungry yesterday, but now she was starving. Usually she drank milk from her mum throughout the day. She ate some of the seaweed from the rock pools, but what she liked most was the sea spinach that was growing all along the coastline. She pulled whole plants up by the roots and ate them, flowers, leaves and all, and when she found some sea kale she ate that too.

Tummies partially filled, Tara and Harvey finally headed back inland towards the rising hills of the Lake District.

By the time Tom and his grandfather reached the shore the two animals were gone.

'What do you think an elephant was doing here?' Tom asked, as he rowed the boat back out to sea to collect their crab pots.

His grandfather didn't know as he hadn't seen what Tom had seen.

'You sure there was an elephant?' he asked. He didn't disbelieve his grandson, but it did seem a bit unlikely.

'Yes!' said Tom.

'Maybe there's a circus coming to St Bees,' his grandfather said mildly. Tom had always been very fond of them.

But Tom shook his head. He'd have known about it if there were. There'd been a circus at Whitehaven, but the last show was yesterday afternoon.

'Do you think it's lost? Maybe we should report it to the police?' he said.

His grandfather didn't think that was a good idea. 'Best leave things be.'

Chapter 9

After Shanti had munched her way slowly through a wheelbarrow full of potatoes, carrots and cabbages, Yolanda, AJ and Mr Jones showed her around the farm.

Standing on the bottom rung of the wooden gate, Yolanda and AJ called to the cows. The inquisitive animals immediately came over to sniff at Shanti. But when she gave a trumpet of greeting one of the cows jumped back in surprise, which made AJ laugh.

'She's only trying to be friendly!' he said.

The sheep, however, didn't come down from the hills when the children called them, and were much more wary of the huge elephant.

Eventually, they started back towards the barn and the cottage. 'Come along, Shanti,' Mr Jones said, turning his chair to follow AJ and Yolanda. He'd only gone a few yards when he was suddenly surprised to find his wheelchair moving along of its own accord. Shanti had taken it upon herself to grip it with the finger-like tips of her trunk and push it just like she'd done with the pram at the circus.

'That's it, Shanti,' AJ said, turning round and laughing at the spectacle.

'Good girl,' said Yolanda. 'Not too fast though.'

'She's surprisingly good at wheelchair pushing,' Mr Jones said, over his shoulder, once he'd got over his shock of having an elephant pushing him. 'This way, Shanti.' He pointed in front of him to show the elephant the way he wanted her to go and Shanti took him past the barn all the way back to the cottage where he pushed himself up the wooden ramp he'd had made to the front door. 'Th-thank you,' he said, feeling slightly shaken by the whole incident, but unable to stop smiling. 'Good elephant,' he said, giving her a pat.

Shanti raised her trunk and opened her mouth for a treat but Mr Jones had nothing to hand so he gave her another pat instead while Yolanda ran inside to find some bread.

'Here you are Shanti,' she said, and the elephant took the loaf from her and ate it in one great gulp.

'Who'd have thought she could push a wheelchair?' AJ said.

'I think there might be quite a lot of things Shanti can do that we didn't know about,' said their dad. 'She is obviously very intelligent and able to think for herself.'

They went inside the house to have their own breakfast, minus any bread.

'I'd rather have porridge anyway,' said Yolanda, and AJ nodded, although he didn't much like its gloopiness. Yolanda was terrible at making porridge, but he didn't ever say so because it would be unkind and he knew that she probably didn't like it either. He didn't think Yolanda liked cooking anything much, but she did it anyway.

After breakfast Mr Jones wheeled himself to his study and over to his desk. There was a picture of Yolanda and AJ's mother hanging on the wall and he looked up at it as he always did.

'You'd be proud of how well our children are doing,' he told her picture. 'And you'd have loved our new pet.'

You should still be here, he thought, as he did every day. He sighed as he picked up a pen and wrote to Jedediah Lewis, the owner of Lewis Brothers' Circus.

Dear Sir,

Your elephant has arrived safely and seems to be settling in well. However I'm puzzled by the note that accompanied her, sadly water damaged so we cannot read most of it, and the mention of the name Tara . . .

'Ready to see what else Shanti can do?' he called to Yolanda and AJ once he'd finished the letter. He headed outside, carrying a handbell he'd brought back from Ceylon. He'd seen people there use a bell to attract elephants' attention and sometimes the elephants wore large cow bells so everyone would know where they were and when they were heading their way.

'Do you think Shanti could help with the apple picking,' Yolanda asked, as they walked back to the barn. The trees were laden with them.

'Shanti does love apples,' AJ said.

'I'm sure she could,' said Mr Jones. 'Although she might eat them all.'

Shanti was munching on her second breakfast of hay in the barn, but she looked up as soon as Mr Jones rang the bell.

'Let's pick some apples, Shanti,' he said, and she followed him and the children to the orchard.

Apple picking, from even the tallest branches, was no problem for Shanti's dextrous trunk. But they didn't go in the fruit-collecting basket – they went in Shanti's mouth.

'Like this, Shanti,' Yolanda said and she dropped an apple in the basket and Shanti copied her and dropped the next apple she picked with her trunk into the basket – and continued to drop those that she didn't eat herself into it.

AJ threw the elephant an apple and was amazed when she caught it with her trunk.

'I bet she's even better at playing ball than Lizzie,' he said. They'd all read about how the people who worked at Tommy Ward's factory had put Lizzie in goal when they were playing football against another team.

Shanti made easy work of picking plums from the tops of the trees too, and no one minded that she ate quite a lot of these as well.

'She's amazing, Dad,' said Yolanda. The fruit picking had taken far less time than it would normally have done.

'What else do you think she could do?' AJ asked.

'Lots of things to help the war effort,' Mr Jones said. 'Maybe she could help transport the trees that need to be cut into logs to help support the trenches at the front and of course help with the ploughing and take the wheat to the mill for grinding. Although I'd never let her push the grindstone. It's too mind-numbing a job for such an intelligent animal. I'd never make Shanti do a job she didn't want to or that I thought she'd hate.'

Once the orchard fruit had been picked Mr Jones and the children went back inside the cottage.

Shanti went back to the barn at first, but then she headed off to the cow field, opened the gate, went inside with the cows and closed the gate after her.

The cows looked over at her but didn't stop eating as she came to join them.

'Would you take this to the post office for me?' Mr Jones asked Yolanda and AJ. 'I want Shanti's previous owner to get it as soon as possible.'

Yolanda and AJ took the letter and headed down the hill from the farm to the village with it.

In the village they met Annie and three of the other women from the WLA who lived in the hostel at the end of the street. They were all dressed up ready for a night out in Whitehaven.

Yolanda had never seen Annie wearing a dress, and a hat with what looked like a recently found pheasant feather in it.

'Are you going somewhere nice?' Yolanda asked the women shyly. The farm women always seemed to be having lots of fun, although she was sure working on the land was very hard work too.

'The music hall at the Royal Standard in Whitehaven,' Annie told her.

Yolanda wished she could go with them. The music hall sounded so glamorous.

'We've got a letter for the Lewis Brothers' ringmaster at the Whitehaven circus ground,' AJ said, and Yolanda told Annie and the other women about the mysterious Tara.

'Shanti got really upset when we said her name,' she finished.

'We'll take the letter for you if you like,' Annie said, and the other women nodded.

'Oh no, it's too much to ask,' Yolanda said. But Annie told her it was no bother at all and took the letter from her.

'Thanks,' AJ said, as the women headed on towards the railway station. The sooner they found out who Tara was the better. Maybe Tara was Shanti's mum or best friend and that was why she'd bellowed so loudly at the sound of her name.

The ringmaster was very surprised when there was a knock at his caravan door a few hours later. His first instinct was not to open it, in case it was one of the many people he owed money to. But when he heard a female voice shouting: 'Anyone in there!' he opened it a crack and peeped out.

'Can I help you, ladies?' he asked, staring at the young woman brandishing an envelope.

Annie handed him Mr Jones's letter. 'Who's this Tara then?' she said.

The ringmaster gulped. 'One minute,' he said, and he closed the door taking the letter with him.

He sat down on a rickety old chair and read: *We've all come to love Shanti and her sweet gentle nature.*

The letter made him feel bad for the way he'd treated the elephant, and even worse when he thought about what could have happened to her daughter. He'd never have separated them if he'd known that Tara might starve. He'd thought Cullen's Circus would have another elephant from which Tara could nurse.

Inside Shanti's headdress we found a note that mentioned 'Tara' and I was wondering who this might be and where she is.

The ringmaster sighed and picked up a letter he had received from Albert instead. Albert had written it on the train from Whitehaven and posted it before he'd got on the boat headed for the Middle East. Every time the ringmaster read the letter it made him feel even more awful about what had happened.

As I leave for Egypt it seems so, so far away from home, but I know you always have my, and the animals', best interests at heart . . . I hope to make you and my father proud.

Albert had also included a letter for Shanti's new owner and asked the ringmaster to forward it to him.

'You going to be long?' Annie called from outside the caravan door.

'One more minute.' The ringmaster sighed even more loudly as he picked up his pen. He'd be off to fight in the war himself soon enough. He'd decided to enlist and this was his last day in Whitehaven. Cullen's Circus would be setting up on the field in a few days' time and he didn't want to be here when they arrived. It was time to tell Albert and Mr Jones the truth.

Back at the farm, Yolanda and AJ were getting Shanti's supper ready.

'She does love her food,' said Yolanda, as she added maize and carrots to the wheelbarrow.

'But I still think Shanti's sad,' AJ said, as he re-filled the elephant's water barrel. It wasn't a sadness you could easily see – not an on-the-top sad. Shanti's unhappiness was buried deep down and didn't always show – but AJ knew it was there. It was like the heavy heartedness he felt when he thought about his mum, who'd died when he was just a baby.

Sometimes when AJ felt low-spirited he liked to go off by himself and play the harmonica his grandad had given him. Tunes from the harmonica always sounded mournful to AJ.

He didn't play it in the house much because Yolanda or his dad would ask him what was wrong. And sometimes he just wanted to have time to feel blue.

He took his harmonica out to Shanti in the barn. Whatever anyone else said, he knew the elephant was sad.

He wasn't taking it out to her to try and cheer her up. He couldn't really even play a tune on it himself apart from 'London's Burning' and a not-quite-right 'Happy Birthday'. He was taking it with him to let Shanti know he knew she was sad and that it was OK for her to be so.

Shanti had eaten all her food and was lying on her side on the straw when he pulled open the barn door. But when he came in she half sat up and then lay back down again.

AJ plonked himself down on a convenient hay bale. Not too near the elephant but not too far away from her either.

He pulled the harmonica from his pocket pressed it to his lips and blew. Shanti's eyes flickered, but she didn't sit up. AJ ran his lips along the harmonica so that all the notes played. He did it again and Shanti's top ear flapped. He tried playing 'London's Burning' and got it almost right and then 'Happy Birthday' and got it mostly wrong.

'AJ,' Yolanda called. 'It's time for dinner.'

And AJ went, leaving the harmonica on the hay bale.

It wasn't much of a stretch for Shanti's trunk to reach the bale, or for her trunk to feel along it until she found the harmonica. Her breath made it play notes even before she'd properly picked it up.

AJ smiled to himself as he ate his burnt stew. In the distance, coming from the barn, he could hear the faint sound of an elephant learning to play a harmonica.

Chapter 10

As Harvey trotted along beside Tara through the green moorland dotted with late summer wildflowers, the railway line never too far away, his instinct told him they were being watched. But whenever he looked round he couldn't see anyone. And whatever it was, it kept downwind of him so his strong sense of smell couldn't identify it.

He whined as Tara turned away from the railway up a rough path to a lake surrounded by brooding mountains. This wasn't the way he wanted to go. He wanted to stick close to the railway tracks, not diverge from them. But Tara wanted to go that way and so he followed her.

Once they were at the lake he couldn't sense whatever had been stalking them any more. But he was still very alert for any slight movement or sound as he lapped at the icy cold, clear glacial water. Tara waded out into the lake, using her trunk to suck up the water and transfer it to her mouth. She lay down in the shallows and then sat up and drank some more. The lake had small waves like the sea had done. But these were gentler – soft ripples.

Harvey put one paw and then the other into the cool water, but he didn't go in any further than that. His paws were sore and had tiny cuts on them from where he'd walked on sharp stones. His legs ached from all the walking, but the wound from where the goad had cut him was healing well.

The sun was warm as it beat down on him, and while Tara finished playing in the water the old dog lay down at the lakeside, closed his eyes and dozed. Eventually, Tara came to join him. At first, she lay on her left side with her legs curled up into her tummy. But then she rolled over on to her right side to try and get more comfortable.

Half asleep now Harvey twitched and whimpered until Tara rested her trunk over him. Then he fell into a deep, deep sleep and he didn't twitch any more. Tara slept too.

The two animals were alone now and far away from the circus. Far away from anything they had previously known.

Suddenly Harvey awoke, his tired body quivering and trembling as his eyes flashed open and he let out a low growl. He'd heard a splash and now his sensitive nose detected the scent of something unlike anything he'd ever smelt before. It wasn't quite a dog or a cat, nor a lion or tiger or camel or horse or any of the other exotic animals he'd smelt during his time at the circus. And yet it wasn't totally dissimilar to them either.

Then he heard a sound, a yipping, almost barking, noise, and he sensed danger close by.

The creature that had followed them was now upwind and Harvey picked up the scent and looked in the direction it was coming from.

There. There it was. Further along by the river that flowed into the lake.

Harvey stood up.

The creature was bigger than him, about the size of a large dog. It had fawn-brown fur with dark stripes across its back and base of its tail.

In its jaws was a salmon and Harvey drooled at the sight of the large fish.

He barked and was surprised when the creature looked over at him, dropped the fish and ran.

Harvey looked down at Tara, still sleeping, and then at the fish, waiting to be eaten and no sign of the creature that had caught it.

He looked back at Tara and whined. The fish was too much to resist. Harvey ran to the salmon and ate and ate until he could eat no more. And all the time he looked back at Tara and over in the direction the creature had fled as he held down the salmon in his paws. He knew the striped wolf-cat must be somewhere near by, probably watching him, but he couldn't see it and it didn't approach again.

Tara woke as Harvey was finishing the fish and gave a cry of utter despair when she couldn't see him. He ran back to her his tail wagging and she trumpeted with happiness.

Together they followed the river that flowed from the lake down into the fells. Harvey cocked his ear as he heard the whistle of a train in the distance.

Tara had never met a sheep before, and now there were sheep with brown fleeces and white faces grazing all around. She stopped to stare at them. But the sheep edged away from her, unsure of the baby elephant, although curious about her too. They stared back at her and bleated once they were a safe distance away.

The lambs fed from their mothers and Tara needed to feed from her mum too. No amount of grass that she ate would be enough to replace it. She needed milk and every day that passed without it left her weaker, hungrier and more disorientated.

That evening the grey clouds that had been lowering all day finally exploded into a storm that ripped through the sky, sending angry raindrops down on the young elephant and the old dog.

Tara's sensitive skin felt every large drop as it landed on her. Harvey tucked his tail miserably between his legs. The rain stung his eyes, but he still looked to the left and right, searching for somewhere to get away from the storm. He needed a place they could both fit. And suddenly he saw it – a darker shadowy area in the rocks just ahead. A cave. He headed towards it, but stopped when he realized Tara was no longer with him. As he looked round for her an almighty thunderclap crashed through the air and he dived into the nearest bramble bush.

Tara, who'd only wandered off a little way, gave a terrified squeal and started running and running in a panic, not knowing where she was going, not caring where she was heading.

Harvey barked at her to stop, but she didn't hear him above the noise of the rain. All she knew was she must run from the sky that had shouted at her. She stumbled and fell heavily, scrambled up again and carried on running.

To the side of her a streak of lightning hit a tree and lit up the landscape as a branch fell to the ground narrowly missing her. Tara swerved to the left and started running that way. But now Harvey saw she was running towards a cliff edge on the wet grass, blinded by the torrential rain and exhausted with panic and lack of proper food.

Harvey barked a warning, but she didn't stop so he ran after her although his chest burned with the pain of running so fast.

To the right of him he saw how to cut her off and just managed to reach the cliff edge and the long drop below it before she did. And there he stood as the wild-eyed baby elephant came running straight at him, ears flapping, and trumpeting in terror.

His old lungs were bursting for air, but he kept his legs braced against the whipping wind and relentless rain. Would she stop? Would she stop in time or would she run right over him? Harvey didn't know, but he wasn't moving. He had to try and stop her.

When Harvey had suddenly gone Tara thought she'd lost him like she'd lost her mum. But now he was standing right in front of her. The little elephant came to a sudden halt when she saw the old dog, almost falling as she did so.

She stretched her trunk out and touched him as if she could hardly believe he was really there. Harvey wagged his tail and licked her face.

He led the little elephant back to the cave through the rain. Here at least they would be dry and safe until the storm passed.

Tara lay down on the cave floor making small whimpering noises. Harvey lay close to her and nuzzled her with his face. He licked her tears away as she cried herself to sleep.

Harvey stared into the darkness listening to the storm raging outside, until cold and aching, his joints stiff, and very uncomfortable on the cave floor, he too fell asleep.

Chapter 11

Mr Jones came to see Shanti in the barn after Yolanda and AJ had gone to Sunday school.

'Morning, sweet Shanti,' he said, as he stroked her trunk. 'What a storm we had last night, didn't wc?' Hc was glad she'd stayed dry in the barn.

Shanti gave a deep rumble as if she were agreeing with him.

The elephant had only been at the farm for a few days, but already Mr Jones found himself thinking of her as part of his family. He knew some people might think him crazy talking to an elephant, but when he looked into her big intelligent eyes he was sure she understood every word. He didn't want her ever to leave.

'Mr Jones?' Annie's voice called, and the next moment she poked her head round the barn door. 'Oh there you are. I've got a letter for you.'

'On a Sunday?'

'It's from the circus ringmaster at Whitehaven. Morning, Shanti.'

She handed the letter to Mr Jones and went to give Shanti a stroke.

'Well, no rest for the wicked. I'm off to help with the bracken bashing – nuisance stuff,' Annie said, as she headed off. She looked over at Mr Jones. He was engrossed in the letter and hadn't even heard her. 'Bye, Shanti.'

Mr Jones unfolded the letter from Albert and frowned at what he read.

*

Everyone at the village Sunday school wanted to know more about the elephant.

'What's her name?'

'How big is she?'

'Can we come and see her?'

'Do you think your elephant would like to eat bracken?' Daisy asked. 'The bracken at the farm needs to be cut back or the sheep can't graze on the grass struggling to grow beneath it.'

'It gets everywhere,' Simon said. 'And it's taller than our sheep now. It's hopeless trying to keep it under control without a horse to pull the bracken basher cart. Even the Land Army girls can't keep it down. It's too much for them.'

'Dad says eating bracken makes farm animals sick,' Yolanda said. 'But I bet Shanti could flatten the bracken for you by pulling the bracken basher.'

Simon and Daisy's eyes lit up.

'Could she?'

'Will you ask your dad?'

'It'd make all the difference to our farm.'

'Ours too,' said some of the other children and Yolanda and AJ promised they'd ask their dad as soon as they got home.

Shanti was in the barn and Mr Jones was in the house when they got back.

'Dad, do you think Shanti would be able to pull the bracken basher like Buttercup and Bluebell used to?' Yolanda asked him.

'What's wrong?' AJ asked. He could see something wasn't right with his dad.

'I've just had a very worrying letter from the ringmaster at Whitehaven, Shanti's old owner,' Mr Jones told them.

He read Yolanda and AJ the letter from the ringmaster telling him who Tara was and that she had run away with a circus dog called Harvey. Then he read them Albert's letter.

It began with helpful training instructions.

Training by ringing a bell when the elephants have done what you want them to do, so that they understand they've got it right is a good idea. It works well for the elephants' best friend, my dog, Harvey, too.

My dad used to say we talk all the time and expect the elephants to listen all the time and then wonder why they don't respond when we tell them to do something.

With a bell ring they'll understand it's training time and be ready to learn. Also, quite often, I find it helps if I do what I want the elephant (or dog) to do first while it's watching and a bit of sign language can also come in very handy.

I hope Tara is not being too much of a handful. She can be a little tinker sometimes and pretend she doesn't know what she's supposed to do when really she does. But that's a two-year-old elephant for you. And I've no doubt you'll love her just like I do. She's still only a toddler really and although she might think she's very grown-up sometimes the truth is she's not old enough to survive for long without her mother's milk.

Anyway, sorry I've gone on for so long – I'm only
trying to help and make it the best possible experience
for you, Shanti and her little daughter, Tara, while
they're with you. Do write back and let me know how
they are getting on if you have a chance. I miss them
more than I can say and can't wait to see them again
once the war is over.
Yours sincerely,
Albert Jennings
Camel Corps.

'So Tara's actually Shanti's baby daughter,'
Yolanda said slowly, as she tried to take in the
awfulness of what had happened. 'Poor Tara.
Poor Shanti. I can't believe it. They should be
together.'

'No wonder Shanti got so upset when we
said her name,' said AJ. Now he knew why she
was so sad. 'But where can her baby be?'

'The circus was at Whitehaven when she
went missing,' Mr Jones said.

'We have to find her, Dad,' Yolanda said, blinking back tears. 'We have to do everything we possibly can to find her and bring her here to live with Shanti and us.'

'We will,' her father promised her. 'We'll go and see Constable Kean right now.'

AJ pushed his father's wheelchair to the front door and so he didn't see the worry on his dad's face. Baby elephants that had been separated from their mothers were very vulnerable and it might already be too late by the time they found Tara. Elephants sometimes gave up and died when they were mourning the loss of their loved oncs and Tara would be particularly susceptible due to malnutrition. But he couldn't tell his children that. It was too awful to even think about.

Shanti heard them from the barn and was waiting at the cottage front door when they came out. She gently nudged AJ out of the way. Pushing Mr Jones's wheelchair was her job. AJ laughed and stepped aside as Shanti held the bar with the end of her trunk and they headed down the hill to the village high street.

A reporter from the local paper came running out of the newspaper office when he saw them. He'd missed Shanti's arrival and was intending to go out to the farm. But now here was the perfect photo opportunity.

'Quick – bring the camera!' he shouted over his shoulder to the photographer. 'This could get us in the national papers!' He hurried forward shouting, 'Sir, sir!'

'Stop, Shanti,' said Mr Jones and Shanti stopped.

'Can we have a picture?' the photographer asked.

'Let's tell them about Shanti's baby,' AJ said and his dad thought this was a very good idea.

They didn't say the name Tara because it was too upsetting for Shanti. They spelt out her name instead.

'We have to find her,' Yolanda said. 'We have to.'

'She's with a Border collie,' said AJ. And he spelt out Harvey's name rather than saying it, just in case Shanti recognized that too.

The reporter wrote it all down and promised the story of the missing baby elephant would be in the paper the next day.

'How about a picture now?' the photographer said, and he took a shot of them all before they headed on up the street to the police station.

Stony Oakhill only had one constable and Constable Kean was a big Shanti fan. He'd met her on the evening she'd arrived and given her a sandwich. Now he brought his leftover strawberry jam sandwiches out with him when he saw her from the station window.

'Well hello, beautiful,' Constable Kean said to Shanti as he patted her.

Shanti opened her mouth wide and Constable Kean popped a jam sandwich inside.

Shanti had already swallowed one sandwich and when she saw that there were more in the brown paper she opened her mouth again.

'Go on then,' Constable Kean said, holding out the bag, and Shanti took out the sandwich using the finger-like tip of her trunk.

'We're here to report a missing elephant,' Mr Jones said.

'Are you? Bit big to mislay isn't it?' Constable Kean joked, until he saw that no one was smiling.

'It's Shanti's baby, T . . .' Yolanda almost said the name but stopped just in time. 'It's spelt T A R A.'

The policeman frowned and almost said the word.

'Don't say it in front of Shanti!' AJ said.

'Oh, of course not,' Constable Kean said, giving Shanti a look. 'So when did *it* go missing?'

'On the day Shanti came to us – three days ago now,' Mr Jones said.

'Have there been any sightings of her?' Constable Kean asked him.

'No – but Shanti only came from Whitehaven,' said AJ.

'Hmmmm, there are miles and miles of open countryside around Whitehaven,' said Constable Kean.

'If we don't find her, she'll die,' Yolanda said. 'She might even be . . .'

'All right,' Constable Kean said, patting her shoulder. 'I'll put the word out and let you know as soon as I hear anything.'

That night, as the previous nights, Shanti bellowed in the barn throughout the evening, but now they knew why.

'Poor Shanti,' Yolanda said to herself as she washed up the dinner plates.

Much later AJ watched from his bedroom window as Shanti headed off down the farm track calling to her daughter with her deep elephant call, but he didn't follow her, and in the morning she'd returned to the barn.

Chapter 12

Tara and Harvey headed through the early morning summer mist across the meadow past the sheep and up the hill. The orchard at the top had plum and apple and pear trees, and Tara hungrily ate the fruit along with the leaves. But here she also found something new – wild strawberries – and the little elephant pulled them up by the runners that grew above ground. A basket of eggs had been left by the front door and Harvey gobbled them up and licked his lips.

In the meadow beyond, Beatrix Potter, wearing a battered old straw hat was painting at an easel. She was visiting a sick friend and thinking how they could really do with a nurse for the villages in the area. How were the farmers supposed to cope when they were ill and the work still needed to be done?

'Oh,' Beatrix exclaimed, when she saw the elephant with a trail of strawberries hanging from its mouth and the old collie dog with her. 'Oh my goodness.'

She'd heard about the missing baby elephant from one of the Land Army girls. Apparently it had been in the paper, but she certainly hadn't expected to see it here of all places. She had to tell someone what she'd seen as soon as possible, so she left her easel and paints where they were, and hurried across the meadow full of daisies and buttercups to the village lane as quickly as she could.

'All right, Miss Potter, I mean Mrs Heelis,' the vicar said as she ran past him.

But Beatrix didn't have time to stop.

Tara and Harvey headed over to the easel that the lady had left, but there was no food there.

Tara picked up one of the paintbrushes with her nimble trunk and dabbed paint on top of the lady's painting of a rabbit wearing clothes.

But by the time Beatrix had come back with the village policeman, Tara and Harvey had travelled on through the meadow and on to the next farm.

The maize growing in the field was almost as tall as Tara and much taller than Harvey. The little elephant had never tasted it before so she did what all elephants do with something new: she touched it with her trunk and then put her trunk in her mouth.

Once she knew it tasted good Tara headed into the field, with Harvey trotting behind her. She broke corn stalks as she ate the corn, which helped Harvey to spot the mice that were in the fields, and so he got to eat too. But the corn wasn't enough for Tara. She had to have her mother's milk. Nothing could replace that and she was getting weaker all the time.

At the end of the field there was a gap in the dry-stone wall and a sloping bank that led down to a river. They wandered down to it. The water looked cool and inviting and Tara waded into it as Harvey crunched through the shell of his first freshwater pearl mussel and watched as a brown trout darted past.

The two animals slept in the sunshine on the riverbank before heading on across another wildflower-covered meadow and out on to a country lane with grass growing down the middle of it.

A curious black-and-white calf came running over to the dry-stone wall as soon as she saw Tara and Harvey on the lane behind it. The calf's mother called to her to come back, but the calf was far too interested in Tara to listen to her. Tara put her trunk over the wall to touch her, and the calf led them along the wall to a rickety wooden gate, which she poked her head through so she could sniff at Harvey. Harvey sniffed back in greeting and wagged his tail.

Tara, Shanti and Harvey were all used to opening doors and gates as part of their circus act and it was no problem at all for Tara to lift up the frayed string that was the only thing keeping this gate shut. She gave the gate a push to open it, whereupon it promptly fell flat on the grass.

Once Tara and Harvey were in the field all the cows and their calves came over. Eventually, when they'd all sniffed and been sniffed at, the cows went back to eating grass and Tara joined them.

It was dusk by the time the farmer came to bring in the cows and he was tired out. Running the farm was too much for an old man and he was dreading the winter. Last year had been terrible. But he had to keep the farm going so his sons had somewhere to return to after the war. They were fighting for their country and he was determined to fight to keep the farm going for them. Only his back ached so much he could hardly straighten it, his head ached, his arms ached, his hands ached and his fingers were twisted with arthritis.

'Come in now, Maisie. Bring 'em in, girl,' he shouted.

And Maisie led the cows and the calves across the field to the cow shed just like she did every night, while the farmer went to check on the gate.

'I'll have to fix this,' he said, and he groaned as he tried to lift it up.

He was very surprised when it suddenly became light as a feather, and even more surprised, as well as scared, when he saw that an elephant was helping him to lift it and put it back in place.

'What – what?' he cried, rubbing his eyes. He'd only ever seen a picture of one before, and he let go of the gate and hurried back to his cottage.

Tara followed the cows and calves as they made their way across the field. Harvey came running out of the bushes, where he'd been munching on a large rat, to follow her.

The cows were eating hay in the shed and Tara ate some too before she found a wheelbarrow full of carrots and ate those instead. There was a tin bathtub full of water for the cows and Tara had a long drink before settling down for the night with the cows and the chickens and farm cats.

The chickens perched on the rafters and the cats stayed clear of Harvey. But the cows and calves lay down together on the straw bedding and Tara made a sad little sound and went to join them. She missed her mum and called out to her using the special elephant call, but Shanti didn't reply.

Maisie licked her with her large pink tongue and Tara lay next to her with Harvey close by.

In the morning Maisie led the cows and calves back out to the field again. Tara and Harvey followed her until they came to the farmer's vegetable garden. There they stopped so Tara could pull up and eat a few cabbages and parsnips while Harvey tried unsuccessfully to catch a toad and had to settle for a worm instead.

The little elephant didn't like the geese that squawked at her and made Harvey bark as they headed after the cows to the field. But she didn't mind the chickens with their funny way of running to catch up with her.

The chickens really liked the baby elephant and followed her about in a little flock wherever she went in the field. The cows and calves cropped the grass by wrapping their muscular tongues round it and pulling it out, but the way Tara ate grass was to loosen it by kicking at the soil with her forefoot. Then she lifted the green grass along with the white roots in her trunk to her mouth. Every time she pulled up the grass by its roots the chickens rushed to the spot where she'd been so they could peck at the ground that she'd softened for insects and worms that had been disturbed.

It was late in the afternoon when Tara heard some music playing across the valley. Curious, she and Harvey went to investigate it.

In Mr Morrison's house, there was a shiny black grand piano in the conservatory, and as the early evening was so warm the conservatory doors had been opened wide.

'Mr Elgar might be playing this tonight after dinner,' Gwen, the young parlourmaid, said to herself as she dusted the piano, excited that the famous composer was visiting her master's house. But for now there was only her in the conservatory, and she'd been taught to play a little by the choir mistress at Chapel.

Gwen sat on the piano stool and ran her fingers lightly over the keys. No one came to see what she was doing, so she played one tune and then another. Tara and Harvey found a hiding place among the trees that edged the garden and watched. But when she started to play Edward Elgar's 'Pomp and Circumstance', one of the circus tunes, Tara gave a *squee* and came out of hiding.

Gwen was so caught up in the music she was playing and trying to remember all the notes that she didn't hear the noise, and for a few seconds she was completely unaware of the little elephant standing at the conservatory doors. She might have made it successfully all the way to the end of the piece had not Tara shuffled forward and plonked her trunk down on the piano keys.

Gwen let out a little squeak, but was too terrified to move.

An elephant. An actual real-life elephant was standing next to her in the conservatory!

Tara plonked her trunk on the notes some more – *bang-bang-bang-bang-bang* – and then she looked at Gwen and plonked her trunk down again. Then she gave the girl a gentle push.

Gwen was sure the little elephant wanted her to play some more and so recovering from her surprise, she did. But not Elgar – one of Scott Joplin's ragtime dances this time, and Tara nodded her head along with the rhythm until she decided to join in too. *Plonk-plonk-plonk*. Then Gwen played another Elgar piece.

'What's all that racket?' An angry voice came from the hall beyond. It was her employer, Mr Morrison. 'Our visitors are trying to get away from the noise of London and certainly don't want to be confronted with it here.'

'I'm sorry, sir,' Gwen said, jumping up as Mr Morrison and Mr and Mrs Elgar entered the conservatory, closely followed by the butler. 'I can play it perfectly. Only –'

Mr Elgar gasped when he saw Tara.

'What on earth is an elephant doing here?'

'It's . . . playing the piano. It isn't doing any harm,' Gwen squeaked helplessly. She felt slightly hysterical.

Tara wiggled her trunk round beside Gwen so she could bash the piano keys once more. *Plonk-plonk-plonk*.

But the butler thought the elephant was doing a lot of harm so he clanged the dinner gong and shouted at Tara, and she ran off, followed by Harvey who had been hovering outside the door.

'It wasn't doing any harm,' said Gwen again, but when she saw the butler glowering she hurried off back to the kitchen.

'I can't believe it,' said Mrs Elgar, laughing.

'We must inform the Buttermere authorities immediately,' Mr Elgar said.

Mr Morrison sent a footman to the police station, and he took the dinner gong with him in case there were any more elephants about that needed to be frightened away.

Half an hour later Gwen was sent for and had to go through the whole incident for the village policeman.

'It joined in with 'Pomp and Circumstance' first, sir,' said Gwen to Mr Elgar.

'And played the piano with its trunk you say?' asked the policeman as he wrote it all down in his notebook.

'Well I wouldn't exactly call it playing, sir,' said Gwen. 'It was more like "plonking".'

'But you can play?' Mr Elgar asked her, smiling, and Gwen told him how she'd been taught.

'The Elgar Elephant,' said Mr Elgar. 'I like the sound of that. Perhaps it should have its own "Little Elephant" tune,' and everyone laughed.

Tara and Harvey headed onwards into the Lake District under a clear starry night and finally fell asleep on some clumps of forest moss close to a bubbling brook.

Around them, the night-time forest animals came out and Harvey listened to their rustles and snuffles as he drifted off to sleep. There was another sound that he listened for now. A sound that often came from Tara. The low elephant call she repeatedly made to her mother. But Shanti never answered her.

Chapter 13

Letters from home arrived at the Front within a day or so of being sent, and Albert had not even fully settled in when he received a letter from the ringmaster.

I'm sorry to inform you that Tara and Harvey have run away together and I can only conclude that the worst must have happened ...

He ran to find his sergeant.

'I have to go home, sir,' he said. 'Tara's life depends on it. I have to help find her. She's still just a baby.'

But when Sergeant Cromer learnt that Tara was an elephant he told Albert in no uncertain terms that he absolutely could not go home and he would be court martialled, and probably shot, if he tried to do so without permission.

'There's a war going on you know, lad. This isn't a picnic.'

Albert worried about the elephants all day and at night he couldn't sleep for worrying. He couldn't understand why Harvey and Tara had run away together. Why wasn't Tara with her mum? She was too young to be separated from her. And what was she doing with Harvey? And why wasn't Harvey with the ringmaster? The elephant and dog shouldn't even be with each other, let alone have run away together.

It just didn't make sense.

As the sun rose across the desert Albert wrote to Shanti's new owner and then he wrote to the ringmaster, although he didn't expect to get a letter back from him. He'd felt that he had been badly let down by the ringmaster, whom he'd trusted completely. Badly let down indeed.

At Forest View Farm, Shanti pushed her head through the special leather harness Mr Hodges the blacksmith had made for her and he tightened the buckles. 'You'll be able to use this for all sorts of jobs from cart work to logging, and of course bracken bashing,' he told Mr Jones, AJ and Yolanda.

Just about every farm in the area had asked if Shanti could help them with bracken bashing. But Daisy and Simon had asked first so their farm was the first to have its overgrown bracken squashed by an elephant.

'But how will you teach Shanti to pull the bracken basher?' AJ asked.

'With lots of apples, carrots and bread,' his dad told him. 'In Ceylon the elephants helped with the forest logging work. I might see if Shanti can help with that, too.'

'How could an elephant help?' AJ asked. Then he grinned. 'Did they chop down the trees?' He laughed as he imagined Shanti with a giant-sized axe. But then he stopped laughing because Shanti with a giant-sized axe would be very dangerous indeed.

'They lifted the logs and sometimes carried the felled trees back to the camp,' Mr Jones told him.

'Mr Soames said we need lots more logs to reinforce the trenches,' Yolanda said.

Mr Jones nodded. 'The elephants in Ceylon had a trainer, known as a mahout, on their backs to show them the way.'

'But we don't have a mahout to help Shanti,' Yolanda said.

'No, so we'll see how Shanti takes to bracken bashing, hay meadow ploughing and forest work. If she likes it, all well and good, but if she doesn't she can still be very useful pulling a cart and transporting heavy things for people around the village.'

'And pushing your wheelchair, Dad,' said AJ.

'Indeed, I bet I'm the only man in England to have a wheelchair-pushing elephant. Maybe even the only man in the whole world to have one,' said Mr Jones.

Mr Hodges attached the bracken-bashing bladed roller to Shanti's harness so she could drag it along behind her to crush and flatten the tough plant stems.

'This way, Shanti, this way,' AJ said, holding out a carrot to show her the way she needed to go.

Bracken bashing was an easy job for the elephant, especially with carrots and windfall apples to coax her along. The fronds of the high bracken scratched softly at her legs as she waded through it.

'That's it, Shanti. Good elephant!' Mr Jones called from the path.

Two hours later the job was done and the invasive bracken had been flattened. They headed to the river so Shanti could cool off and have a bath. The people were hot too, and the children went swimming in the river with Shanti while Simon and Daisy's mum sat on the riverbank with Mr Jones.

'She's made such a difference,' Daisy's mum said. 'Now the plants that were struggling beneath the bracken will have a chance to grow.'

'Shanti could help with the ploughing too,' Yolanda shouted from the river. 'Couldn't she, Dad?'

'She certainly could,' said Mr Jones as Shanti squirted water over herself with her trunk and the children got soaked too.

'Yeew!' Daisy squealed and laughed.

The next moment the children were splashing Shanti with water and she was squirting them back.

'I'm so glad Stony Oakhill got to have its own village elephant,' Simon said, his eyes shining, when the children finally came out of the river and lay on the riverbank to dry while Shanti pulled up grass with her trunk and ate it.

While they were there, Shanti made her elephant call.

'She's calling out to Tara, isn't she?' Yolanda whispered to her dad.

And Mr Jones nodded. 'If either one of you were lost I would never stop calling until I found you,' he said.

Shanti wasn't the only one trying to find Tara. Constable Kean was looking for her too. He visited Gwen and saw the piano that the little elephant had played, heard about how Beatrix Potter had seen her one morning, and listened as a farmer told him about his crushed maize.

'Looked like a herd of elephants had gone through it, not just one young one. Left a few footprints in the mud. Come on, I'll show you.'

Constable Kean went to see the footprints. They definitely looked as if an elephant had made them.

'If it isn't an elephant, I don't know what kind of beast it could be,' the farmer said. 'You don't think it could be the Vampire Dog of Ennerdale come back, do you?'

Constable Kean shook his head. The stripy backed Vampire or Girt Dog of Ennerdale had been killed more than a hundred years ago, but people were still thinking they'd spotted it. Girt Dogs and Zeppelins – people were always reporting seeing one or the other of them, but there never seemed much evidence for the sightings when he went to investigate. He wished people would get out and look for the little elephant instead.

The local newspaper's piece had come out on the day after they'd learnt about Tara and it had immediately been reprinted in the evening edition of the national newspapers. It was just the sort of story they were looking for to lighten the sombre times and they added a cartoon strip of Tara peeping out of one of the windows of Buckingham Palace and at Brighton Pier and on top of the Albert Memorial.

'That's my elephant!' Albert told the other men in the camel corps, when the newspaper was delivered to them, as he went to clean up the camel droppings. But the truth was he wanted Tara to be found very soon. He wanted her to be safe and well-fed and back with her mum before it was too late.

In America the escapologist and illusionist Harry Houdini read about Tara's plight over his morning coffee. Just about everyone who read a newspaper now knew the little elephant's name. He smiled at the cartoon strip showing a missing Tara hiding in different famous landmarks.

'You'd have imagined it would be almost impossible to hide an elephant,' he said to himself. 'Unless it was done as an illusion trick of course . . .' He started making notes, wondering how a disappearing elephant trick might work.

'Maybe it wouldn't be impossible after all,' he said, looking at his notes an hour later, and taking a swig of his now stone-cold coffee.

Chapter 14

Sheep were wary of Tara, although they watched her when she wasn't too close. But the six saddleback piglets on a farm not far from the railway track at Keswick weren't the least bit frightened and came running over and squealing as soon as they saw her. Harvey wagged his tail, but the pigs had seen dogs before – Tara was the one they were interested in. The piglets' mother broke into a trot as she followed them and Tara made her happy squee trumpet noise as the piglets squealed excitedly.

The little pink-and-black piglets and their mother had a field with trees at one end, a dry sty to sleep in, and a boggy pond for mud baths. Tara headed straight over to the pond with the piglets trotting along beside her. As soon as they realized where their visitor was headed they all wanted to join in and raced to be first.

There was just enough room for everyone to fit in the pond, although it was a bit of a squeeze. The pigs and Tara were soon covered in sticky mud, helped in part by Tara squirting it over herself and them. Harvey sat on the bank – he wasn't tempted to have a mud bath.

Bathtime over, the piglets ran in and out of the trees and around Tara while Harvey and the mother pig lay down under a tree in the afternoon sun. Tara seemed to have a little less energy with every day that passed now. But she joined in the piglets' game with enthusiasm. However, she didn't last as long as the piglets did and she soon needed to lie down under a tree and have a sleep. It was five days since she and Harvey had run away from the circus, and Tara was really starting to suffer without her mother's milk now.

Harvey wagged his tail when he saw two much larger and heavier dogs running across the pig field towards him. He lay down to show them that he wasn't a threat, but they came straight at him, slathering and snarling.

Harvey might, in his younger days, have been able to take on one of the dogs. But not two of them at once, and certainly not now he was old and hungry.

He curled into a ball to protect his belly and throat as the dogs attacked him.

Tara saw the dogs coming too, and got up from under her tree. When they started hurting her friend she shook her head in a display of intimidation then charged at them. From somewhere deep within her came a threatening deep trumpeting roar rather than her normal happy *squee*.

The dogs ran away from the angry elephant, leaving Harvey bitten and bleeding. He hobbled out of the field whimpering in pain with Tara beside him. But neither he nor Tara were strong enough to go far any more. Harvey was bleeding badly and the fight and playing with the pigs had used up all of Tara's strength. They eventually stopped and lay down under some bushes not far from the farm.

Tara nuzzled her head against her friend and Harvey finally fell asleep. When he woke up a little later, crying out in pain, Tara gently laid her trunk over the old dog to comfort him, and they both slept.

Every summer for as long as he could remember in all his eleven years, Ezra, and his sister Sadie, younger by two years, had travelled to the

Appleby Horse Fair with their grandmother in their caravan. Not that they had any horses to sell this year. The army had requisitioned all the single-colour horses and they needed Tilly, the piebald, to pull the caravan. Tilly would probably have been taken too, only the cavalry officers didn't want to ride a black-and-white horse. Ezra was very glad about that because he didn't think Tilly would like going off to war, not one little bit.

Ezra's older brother, Gregor, was fighting in France. He'd signed up almost as soon as the first call for men to enlist had gone out. People said gypsy men wouldn't join the fight. But they were wrong about that. Ezra hadn't heard from Gregor in a long time now. His grandmother told Ezra and his sister not to worry, and Ezra tried not to, but he couldn't help it. And he was sure his grandmother was worried too. She just wouldn't say so because that's what his grandmother was like.

This year they'd stayed in the local area after the fair for far longer than usual. There didn't seem to be a reason for rushing away any more and they were only just starting to make their way back across the country now.

It was a very hot day again and Ezra was giving Tilly a bath in the river to cool her off when he heard a high-pitched sound. He looked round and was amazed to see a baby elephant coming through the trees accompanied by a black-and-white dog that was limping. The little elephant splashed its way into the river and had a long drink while the injured dog lay on the riverbank and watched.

Ezra looked behind them to see who they were with, but he couldn't see anyone.

Tilly was a bit spooked by the elephant because she'd never met one before. Ezra stroked her nose to soothe her. 'It's OK, it's OK, my lovely,' he said, as he headed towards the baby elephant, but not too close. He'd never met one before either.

Harvey gave a bark of warning to Tara followed by a whine because even barking hurt him now. Tara rolled over in the water until she was completely submerged apart from her trunk sticking out.

Ezra let go of Tilly who immediately headed out of the river and went over to sniff at the dog, who sniffed back at her and tried to wag his tail.

'Hello,' Ezra said to Tara, holding out his hand to her. Tara poked her head up out of the water and stretched out her trunk to him. She followed him out of the river to sit on the bank in the warm sun. Harvey pushed his head under Ezra's hand to encourage him to stroke him and Ezra happily obliged.

'You're a good dog you are,' he said, as Harvey looked up at the boy with dark hair and even darker eyes, his skin tanned by the long summer days. A good dog, who could do with his help, Ezra decided. He could see the dog's wounds needed cleaning and suspected a good meal wouldn't do him any harm either.

Tara put her trunk in Ezra's pocket to see if he had any treats.

'You hungry too?' Ezra asked her. He decided to take the elephant and dog back to the caravan and give the baby elephant some milk from Rosie, their cow.

'Come on,' he said, taking Tilly's reins, and the elephant and dog followed him as he led Tilly back to the caravan. He was disappointed when he saw that his sister wasn't there and his gran was fast asleep. He knew better than to disturb her when she was napping.

Ezra grabbed the metal bucket they used for milking while Tara and Harvey lay down to watch him and Tilly cropped the long grass at the side of the road.

It wasn't Rosie's usual time for milking.

'Please, Rosie, just a little bit of milk,' Ezra said. 'It's for a hungry baby elephant.'

He was just about to give the milk he'd collected to Tara when his grandmother's sharp bony fingers grabbed his wrist.

'No, Ezra! Cow's milk will kill it,' she told him. 'Baby elephants should never be given cow's milk. Just like foals shouldn't.'

'So what can she have to drink?' Ezra said. He felt angry with his gran for telling him off and scared that he'd nearly hurt the little elephant by trying to help her.

'No milk other than elephant's milk, or maybe a little coconut milk. Yes, I'm sure I've heard coconut can be good, and honey. I've heard of people giving an elephant some honey. And vegetables and fruit, lots of vegetables and fruit.'

'Right,' Ezra said, he knew how to get honey. But as for coconuts . . .

'In the meantime I'll make it some hay mash. You see if you can catch some rabbits for that hungry-looking dog and gather some moss for his wounds. And then you can tell me where you found these two.'

Ezra hurried off while his grandmother poured water and hay and honey and herbs into the cooking pot on the fire.

Sadie could hardly believe it when she came back from selling pegs to find an elephant in their small camp.

'A real-life elephant,' she said, as she stroked Tara's trunk. 'Can we keep her?'

But her grandmother shook her head. 'An elephant needs to be with other elephants,' she said.

When the hay porridge was cool Ezra poured it into a bucket for Tara, and Tara put her trunk in the bucket and lifted the mash to her mouth and ate a little of it while the children and their grandmother watched.

'Good,' Ezra's grandmother said. 'Very good.'

And then she turned back to the fire to make rabbit stew for them and Harvey. Harvey had two bowls full and licked them clean. Only then did Ezra's grandmother carefully clean his wounds and bandage his paw. Harvey knew he could trust the wrinkled old woman's experienced hands, and he let her treat him even though some of his wounds were very painful. When she touched a particularly sensitive spot he made a little sucking sound and the old woman nodded as if she knew exactly what he meant.

'Looks like you found them in the nick of time,' Ezra's grandmother told him. 'Lucky you saw them and brought them here.'

Ezra smiled. The flames from the fire made flickering shadows across Tara's face as they all sat round it. Ezra's grandmother had put a colourful warm blanket round the little elephant, for comfort more than anything else.

'She should be with her mother,' Sadie said.

Their grandmother poked at the fire. 'She should,' she agreed.

'Do you think . . . do you think her mother is dead?' Ezra asked.

His grandmother used a stick from the flames to light the pipe she liked to smoke in the evenings before replying. 'An elephant's bond with its family is as strong as our gypsy bond. Her mother would never willingly have let her go and this little one would never have run from her unless something very bad happened.'

'So do you think –'

But his grandmother didn't let him finish.

'At least she has the dog to watch out for her. He's a good friend.'

Tara's eyelids were drooping and a moment later she'd fallen fast asleep and was making snuffling sounds as she dreamt.

Harvey lay beside her, trying to stay awake but his eyelids were drooping too. The warmth of the fire and the comfort of the blanket that he shared with Tara, together with his full belly, coupled with the soft kind voices around him, made Harvey drift off to sleep too, lying close to his friend. Safe at last.

When Ezra picked up the violin and began to play, the lilting music didn't wake Harvey, but it drifted into Tara's dream and her eyes flickered open and her trunk swayed from side to side almost as if it were dancing.

'She likes it,' Ezra said.

'Most animals love music,' his grandmother told him as she looked over at Tilly and Rosie who had turned to watch him play. 'Let the little elephant sleep now. Tomorrow you will play again.'

Ezra put down the violin and Tara was soon in a deep sleep once more.

Chapter 15

The next morning Tara woke to find herself snuggled up in a soft knitted blanket that felt almost like being hugged.

Harvey was already awake and having his wounds checked by Ezra's grandmother.

'Looking good,' she said, nodding at Harvey. 'Good healing power for an old dog.'

Harvey licked the old woman's liver-spotted hand.

For breakfast there was more warm hay-and-honey mash for Tara and leftover stew from the night before for Harvey. Once that was eaten, Tara headed to the river, followed by the children and Harvey, who was never far from the little elephant's side.

Soon Ezra, Sadie and Tara were in the middle of a wild game with Ezra and Sadie splashing the water at Tara and Tara squirting water back at them with her trunk.

Harvey looked from one of them to the other as Tara gave her distinctive happy squee trumpet sound and the children laughed and squealed.

Back at the caravan later, Sadie practised her scarf dance for the next gypsy gathering while Ezra accompanied her on his violin. Tara watched as the scarf floated and twirled through the air. It had tiny thin fake coins sewn round the edges, which made jingling sounds as the scarf moved. Tara was desperate to join in and kept trying to pluck the scarf away from Sadie with her trunk.

'No, little elephant!' Sadie laughed, skipping away from her. But that only made Tara want the scarf even more.

Finally their grandmother found another scarf for Tara and the little elephant tossed it up in the air and caught it and twirled it in circles with her trunk as she'd once done with the yellow ribbon in the circus ring. Ezra played a new tune and Tara made the scarf swirl back and forth as Sadie danced around her.

After lunch they hitched the caravan up to Tilly. It was time to move on.

Harvey rode with Ezra and Sadie's grandmother at the front of the caravan and Tara walked with the children. She still had the scarf and wouldn't give it back when Sadie went to take it from her. Now she held it in her trunk or laid it on her back as if it were a cloak.

'There might be a coconut shy at Mardale village fete,' Sadie said, as they passed a handwritten sign stuck to a post in the ground. 'We could try and win one for Tara.'

'Gypsies aren't welcome in Mardale,' their gran said.

But Ezra badly wanted to win a coconut for Tara.

'Please, Gran,' he said. 'We'll be in and out of the fete before anyone realizes what we are.'

His grandmother sighed loudly, but turned the caravan down the road for Mardale.

'I'll wait for you here by the trees,' she said. 'But be quick and be careful.' She held out the few coins she had and Ezra took them.

'Thanks, Gran.'

'Just don't get into any trouble.'

'I won't.'

Tara tried to follow Ezra and Sadie.

'No, little elephant, you wait here,' their grandmother said and offered Tara some windfall apples. She was soon busy eating them and the children hurried off.

The fete was being held on the village green and there were lots of people there. Ezra and Sadie passed the bowling-for-a-pig stall, a Punch and Judy show, a small woodwind orchestra that was playing off-key, a ferret race and people knocking over skittles.

'Can you see the coconut shy?' Ezra said.

'No . . . Yes! . . . Over there!'

They hurried over to the stall at the far side of the fete.

It had eight coconuts balanced on top of wooden posts and a queue of people wanting to pay their money and be given three goes to try and knock one of them off. Ezra and Sadie joined the end of the queue as a boy and a girl took it in turns to throw the hard balls at the coconuts.

In front of Ezra and Sadie was a young red-headed soldier.

'There you are, sir,' said the stallholder handing the soldier three wooden balls when his turn came. 'Best of luck to you.'

The soldier took careful aim with each ball, but he didn't manage to knock a coconut off.

'Another go,' he said, handing over more money and getting more balls.

But even though he had two more goes, and did seem to hit a couple of the coconuts right in the centre, none of them fell to the ground.

'The coconuts look like they're stuck on those posts,' Sadie whispered.

Ezra nodded. But he handed over the money to the stallholder anyway and was given three hard balls.

His first ball struck hard, right in the centre of a coconut.

'A direct hit!'

'Good shot!' said the soldier, who'd stayed to watch.

But although the post wobbled and the coconut looked as if it should have fallen, it didn't drop.

'I told you,' Sadie said. 'They're stuck on!'

'How dare you!' the stallholder shouted, sounding really angry and going red in the face. 'Go on – be off with you. Gypsies like you shouldn't be allowed here anyway.' He clenched his fist.

'Steady on now,' said the soldier.

Ezra desperately wanted to win a coconut for Tara.

'But I still have two more balls to throw,' he said, holding them out for the stallholder to see.

'No – no more goes for you!'

'Please . . .'

But the stallholder turned away from him.

'Let me have another go, then,' said the soldier, and he winked at Ezra.

The stallholder took his money and handed him three balls. But even though the soldier hit one of the coconuts as hard as he could it still didn't fall off its stand.

By this time there was quite a crowd, and more people noticed how hard it was to knock down the coconuts. At first there were quiet grumbles about it not being fair, but soon the grumbles grew louder.

'It's your fault,' the stallholder growled at Ezra. 'Thieves and troublemakers the lot of you. Go on, be off now.'

Wherever they went there were some people who hated them because of the lives they led.

Ezra didn't want to leave the coconut shy, but his grandmother had warned them not to get in any trouble. Sadie took his hand.

'Come on,' she said.

They passed a poster advertising 'Cullen's Circus Extravaganza coming to Whitehaven soon' and had almost left Mardale village fete when there was a shout.

'Hey, gypsy boy!'

Ezra stopped, his heart thumping fast. Sadie's face went pale.

'This is for you,' the soldier said, catching up with them. He handed Ezra a coconut.

'It should have been yours. You won it fair and square.'

Ezra couldn't believe it. 'Thank you,' he said. 'Thank you very much indeed.' He'd expected trouble, but for once had met kindness instead.

'You must really like coconuts,' the soldier grinned.

'Never even tasted one,' Ezra said. 'And I doubt I'll taste this one either.'

'Is it for you then?' the soldier asked Sadie.

Sadie shook her head. 'It's for a baby elephant,' she said, before she saw Ezra's warning look and clamped her mouth shut.

'Like the missing one in the newspaper? The one with the cartoon strip?' the soldier asked them.

'Got to go,' Ezra said, and the two of them ran off as fast as they could, back to the caravan with the coconut.

Chapter 16

Tara made her squee trumpet noise when she saw Ezra and Sadie heading towards the caravan and Harvey wagged his tail.

'Here, little elephant, look what we got for you,' Ezra said, as he broke the coconut with a hammer and collected the flesh and milk in a bowl.

Tara picked up a piece with her trunk and took it to her mouth, but then dropped it on the ground.

'Go on, Tara, it's good,' they encouraged her. But Tara didn't want to eat.

'Please, little elephant,' Ezra begged. 'Just drink the milk.' He tried breaking the coconut up into smaller pieces, but still she wouldn't touch it and that night she wouldn't eat the hay porridge either.

'It's like she's given up,' said Sadie when Tara refused to eat anything and only drank a little water the next morning.

'She's been without her mother for too long. A baby elephant needs its mother and it needs elephant milk,' their grandmother told them. She was now very worried indeed. The little elephant had started to rock back and forth as she tried to comfort herself. Her skin was looking dull and very thin and the old woman was sure she was dehydrated as well as malnourished, despite their best efforts. The situation was dire. 'She needs her mother,' she said again. But they had no idea where the little elephant's mother might be.

Ezra told his grandmother what the soldier said about there being a missing baby elephant in the paper. 'Should we take her to the police?'

But his grandmother shook her head. 'The police will only accuse us of stealing her.'

'There's a circus coming to Whitehaven,' Sadie said. 'We saw a poster for it at the fete.'

'Maybe it's the circus our baby elephant came from,' Ezra said, hoping against hope. 'Maybe somehow she got lost or left behind.'

'Let's take her there,' their grandmother said. 'Let them hand her in. At least the circus should know more about baby elephants than we do.'

Tara wore the knitted blanket on her back as they travelled slowly down the country lanes back towards Whitehaven and Cullen's Circus. She was cold and shivery and even turned away from the apples that were offered her.

Harvey came down from the caravan step he liked to sit on with Ezra and Sadie's grandmother to walk with her and the children.

The little elephant was no longer interested in the other animals in the fields they passed. A cow mooed over a fence to her and she didn't even look up. A pheasant flew right in front of her and she didn't even seem to notice it because her head was so drooped.

Harvey looked at his friend and whined.

'She's so sad and she needs her mum,' said Sadie as Tara stumbled to her knees and then staggered up again. She didn't even seem to know where she was any more as she stared into the distance half dazed.

'We have to get her to the circus at Whitehaven before it moves on,' Ezra said.

But Tara could no longer go very far before she had to rest.

'She's getting sicker all the time,' Sadie said, her voice catching in her throat.

'Hush now, we're doing everything we can,' her grandmother told her.

But no one was really sure if everything they could do would be enough. The little elephant had grown so weak so quickly, despite their best efforts. It seemed very much like she'd given up even trying to live.

Harvey stayed close and licked his friend as she shivered and whimpered.

'Come on, little elephant, come on,' Sadie and Ezra encouraged, as they tried to coax her onwards when she lay down in the grass and didn't want to get up.

Harvey whined and nudged at her with his silver-whiskered muzzle and finally she stood up and staggered forwards only for her legs to buckle as she crumpled to the ground.

'Come on, little elephant, you have to eat, you have to drink, you have to walk . . .' the children and their grandmother told her as

Tara lay on the cool, wet grass. But all Tara wanted to do was sleep, and all Harvey wanted was to be there beside her, whining sometimes and licking her ears occasionally, but mostly just there to comfort her by being close.

'How much longer until we get to Whitehaven?' Ezra asked his grandmother.

'One day if we hurry, but probably two at the pace we've been going at.'

They looked at each other and hoped.

'We'll camp here under the trees for tonight,' their grandmother said, as she peered up at the sky. It looked as if there was another storm coming. They made a fire and Sadie and Ezra picked wild strawberries for Tara to try and tempt her to eat, but she just turned her head away.

Ezra, Sadie and their grandmother were fast asleep when Harvey put his paw out to Tara and whined softly to wake her.

The little elephant was so much thinner than when they'd left the circus seven days ago, and very weak. But she did her best to follow her friend as he led her away across the field beneath the moonless sky.

He led her towards the distant railway tracks they'd been following before Ezra had found them. His instinct was telling him this was the way to find her mum. Above them the clouds covered the sky and hid the moon and stars. Tonight it was very dark and even if Tara hadn't been so weak the two animals would have stayed close. Tara was cold all the time and shivered beneath her knitted blanket.

When the lightning suddenly crashed through the sky followed by a roar of thunder the little elephant cried out in fear and started to run, the blanket slipping from her back, her ears flung back. She called out to her mum, but Shanti didn't reply. She never replied.

Harvey barked at her to stop as the rain started to come down. She was too tired to keep on going and he was able to catch up with her and guide her towards the shelter of the trees ahead.

Then an even bigger flash of lightning lit up the whole of the sky, followed by a boom of thunder.

Tara screamed in terror and started to run again, but tripped and fell over a tree branch. But this time, finally, Tara heard a call so strong that its vibrations ripped through the countryside. And Tara let out a squeal of surprise and joy as the rain splashed down on her. Her mum. It was her mum. Her mum at last! Tara stood up and lifted her trunk and with every fibre of her weak little elephant's body quivering with excitement she called back with her own deep elephant call that only her mother could hear.

The next moment she was running as fast as she could through the storm to find her mother. There was Shanti's call again from this side and then from that and always kilometres away but Tara knew she had to reach her. Each time she heard it Tara spun and ran in the new direction that it came from, but the heavy wind and the lashing rain took the elephant's call and distorted it as it threw the sound through the sky.

Harvey ran after the little elephant, barking at her to slow down and wait for him. But Tara only had ears for her mum's call.

Harvey panted as he ran after her. He was determined not to lose her although his paw was now bleeding again and his old lungs felt like they were bursting as he gasped for air.

Tara finally stopped running when she came to the edge of a huge lake that stretched between her and where her mum was calling to her from, somewhere over on the other side of it. It looked further than she'd ever swum before, so far that in the rain she couldn't even see the other side, and it was very dark. But she waded into the cold water and started to swim.

And Harvey, who'd always been afraid of water, went in after her.

Chapter 17

The flash of the lightning woke AJ. This summer storm was even more violent than the one last week, and that had been bad enough. AJ didn't like storms at all and he pulled the bed covers up around his chin and then over his head, wishing it would stop.

But then he thought of Shanti and wondered if she was frightened too. She was all alone out there in the barn and missing her baby. Just because she was big didn't mean she couldn't be frightened too. AJ wrapped a blanket round himself and ran down the stairs, out of the front door and into the darkness.

The rain was so heavy that it was hard to see where he was going, but fortunately he knew the way to Shanti's barn with his eyes shut.

The door had come unlatched and was creaking and banging as it swung to and fro.

'Shanti?' AJ called, as he went inside the barn. 'Shanti, are you OK? I'm here now. It's all right. You're safe.'

Shanti usually came over to him straight away when he went into the barn. But not tonight.

'Shanti?' AJ said, his voice quavering and a sense of dread growing inside him as he realized the elephant wasn't there.

'Shanti!' he shouted. 'Shanti!' And he ran back to the house.

Yolanda was waiting for him at the door.

'What are you doing out in the rain?' she asked him as he came in drenched to the skin.

'It's Shanti – she's gone!' he cried.

Shanti's feet thundered across the wet earth as she ran towards the sound of her daughter's cries. She called to her again wanting to get a more exact location, but Tara didn't call back. Shanti gave a bellow of despair and raced on, crashing through the wooden farm gates that led down to the lake.

The current in the lake was so strong that Tara's head kept bobbing under the water as she tried to fight against it. But it was so hard to keep swimming and the lake water was so very very cold and Tara was so tired. When she sank beneath the water she desperately stuck her trunk up like a snorkel, but still she kept sinking beneath the surface and gulping down great mouthfuls of water.

She couldn't go on any further. She was too weak and the cold was too much to bear and her legs stopped treading water as she cried out.

Shanti bellowed back to her as she waded into the lake and began to swim to her daughter. Harvey clambered on to a piece of floating driftwood and barked and barked. Shanti heard his barks, and her elephant's bellow rang through the air.

Even from below the water, Tara heard and felt her mum's call. She lifted her trunk and kicked her legs upwards until her head came out.

And Shanti's bellow turned to a cry of utter joy.

It was too far for Tara to swim to the mainland, but with Shanti pushing the exhausted little elephant through the water they swam to the nearby shoreline of one of the many uninhabited islands in the lake. Harvey slipped off the driftwood to follow them just as the storm stopped, as suddenly as it had started.

As soon they could stand up in the water mother and daughter elephant wrapped their trunks round each other. Tara was very weak and Shanti had to help by nudging her to the shore.

Once they were there Tara nuzzled her head against her mum. Harvey came out of the water and although he, too, was exhausted, he spun round and round like a puppy for joy. They'd found Shanti at last.

Shanti kept touching her daughter with her trunk and wrapping her trunk round her as if she couldn't quite believe it was true, while all the time the elephants made happy sounds as Harvey lay down and watched the two of them, his tail thumping up and down.

Now Tara was at last able to have the mother's milk that she so desperately needed. And Shanti had her daughter back and she trumpeted to the ethereal Northern Lights that flickered and danced across the night sky. Once Tara had had enough milk the two elephants lay down under the cover of the trees to rest.

Tara slept that night curled up next to her mum, their trunks wrapped around each other, and in the morning when she woke up her mum was still there and she gave a soft squee of pure happiness as she cuddled up to her and then went back to sleep.

Chapter 18

Back at the farm, Yolanda, AJ and their father were beside themselves with worry. They'd been up the whole night and none of them felt like eating the porridge that Yolanda had made for breakfast.

'But where can they be?' AJ said desperately, as he stirred the rapidly cooling gloop.

'The storm was so bad last night and the lightning . . .' Yolanda said, looking over at her dad, but not daring to say what it was that she'd been dreading. Shanti was so big, and she wasn't exactly nimble. What if she'd been struck by the lightning? What if she was lying injured somewhere? Crying out to them. The Lake District could be a very dangerous place in a storm.

'Cooee!' Annie called coming into the cottage. 'All ready for Shanti to have a go at logging?' She stopped when she saw the three of them. 'What's wrong?'

'Shanti's gone missing,' Yolanda told her.

Annie, as always, was immediately practical. 'Right, I'll get the rest of the girls on the search and let Constable Kean know. We'll have a search party out looking for her and I bet we'll have found her by lunchtime. After all, how difficult can it be to find a giant-sized elephant?'

AJ wanted to say that they hadn't had much luck with finding the baby one, but he held his tongue because that would be mean, and Annie only wanted to help.

'Thank you, Annie,' Mr Jones said. He was feeling very low. Lower than he could remember in a long time. 'We'll stay here.'

'In case she comes back,' AJ said. He wanted that more than anything in the world.

But Shanti didn't come back that day and although the Women's Land Army searched high and low they couldn't find her.

'Have you seen an elephant?' Annie asked everyone she met. But no one had. Not today.

'The storm's ripped my gate right off its hinges,' a farmer told them, looking at the wooden gate through which Shanti had crashed. Annie and two of the other women helped by holding the gate in place as he banged in new hinges with a hammer.

Annie looked over at Windermere just beyond his farm. The lake looked so beautiful now the sun had come out, but she wouldn't have wanted to be out on it during last night's storm.

*

Over on the uninhabited island, Tara mostly ate and slept while Shanti stayed close and was never more than a few steps away from her daughter. Her trunk often reached out to touch her baby softly as if she still couldn't quite believe she'd got her back.

Harvey slept too. Long deep sleeps where he snored loudly and twitched, before waking with a joyful wag of his tail because the three of them were back together.

For the next two days they stayed on the island. Tara continued to build up her strength, and once Shanti was sure her daughter was strong enough to swim again she took Tara and Harvey home.

AJ was the first to see the two elephants, one large and one small, accompanied by an old collie dog, heading down the farm path. He'd been looking out of his bedroom window and hoping that Shanti would come home, and now she had.

'Shanti's come home,' he shouted as loudly as he could. The news was so good that it was bursting from him. 'She's come home – and she's not alone!'

Yolanda dropped the soup pot she was washing up and came running out of the house. The children raced down the farm path towards Shanti and Tara and their friend Harvey.

When they reached them, Yolanda threw her arms round Shanti and burst into tears, then found she couldn't stop.

'It's just that I've missed her so and we were so happy when she was here,' she said, as she mopped at her eyes. 'And then we went back to just the same as we used to be and I miss Mum so much and . . .'

'I know,' AJ said softly. 'I feel the same.'

Harvey wagged his tail, worried by Yolanda's tears and then he licked her hand. She stroked him as Tara gave a little squee and ruffled up AJ's hair.

'Good to have you home again, Shanti,' said Mr Jones, coming down the farm path in his wheelchair. Harvey pushed his head under the man's hand so he could stroke him and Tara went to ruffle his hair, but Shanti stopped her with a rumble. The big elephant reached out her trunk and pushed Mr Jones back towards the barn.

'I bet she's hungry,' AJ said, when Shanti stopped outside it, lifted up her trunk and opened her mouth.

'Elephants are always hungry!' Yolanda laughed, as she brushed away the last of her tears, and they ran to fill the wheelbarrow.

That evening, Mr Jones wrote to Albert to let him know that Tara and Harvey had been found and were now living at the farm too.

As I'm sure you know, Tara means star, and that little elephant of yours must have been born under one very lucky star to have found her mother, with the help of your dog Harvey, just in time . . .

Chapter 19

Shanti, Tara and Harvey often went into the village with AJ, Yolanda and their dad. The animals had been living at Stony Oakhill for almost two years now and were used to being made a big fuss of by the villagers whenever they went there. But this June day there were even more villagers about than usual.

Every year Stony Oakhill had a fund-raising fete on the village common, and it was being held today, the union jack flag bunting stretching all round the stalls proclaiming the victory that had happened on the eleventh of November the year before in 1918.

When the elephants arrived, Tara looked up at the little flags fluttering in the wind. She raised her trunk and gave a gentle tug at the flag nearest to her. But the string wasn't designed to withstand an elephant's pulling, even a baby elephant's, and a whole section of the bunting fluttered down to become Tara's new toy.

'Oh no,' said Yolanda. The beautiful display was ruined as all the flags that had been pinned to the stalls with the string fell down.

But the next moment the villagers and fete-goers were smiling as Tara swung her new bunting toy back and forth. She twirled it around herself giving little squeals of delight.

'Isn't she sweet.'

'How absolutely adorable.'

'Quick, take a picture of her for the newspaper!'

The local newspaper photographer was kept busy using his pocket Kodak to take snaps of the fete-goers with the elephants for a penny a time. Fortunately the two elephants seemed more than happy to have their pictures taken and be given a stroke or a pat by the person being photographed for half a bun each.

Mr Jones kept a watchful eye on them from the side to make sure everything went smoothly and that the elephants had a break every now and again.

'She's such a poppet,' people said, as they stood next to Tara.

Tara's tuft of thicker fur on the top of her head gave her a cute, slightly comical, look in the pictures.

'Can we have our picture with both of them?'

'Certainly.'

'Do they give rides?' a man asked.

Mr Jones told him that they didn't.

Beatrix Potter could not resist getting out her watercolours and painting a picture of Shanti and Tara while the people were having their photographs taken with them.

'I saw them when they were in the circus at Whitehaven, you know,' she told Yolanda and AJ. 'I told my husband, Mr Heelis, we were in for a treat that afternoon and we were. Made me think I'd like to write a story about a circus one day.'

When Tara saw what Beatrix was doing she wanted to have another go at painting too. She came over and took the paintbrush from her and dabbed it at the canvas to create her own splodgy painting on top of Beatrix's, but Beatrix didn't mind.

Mr Heelis came over to say hello and Tara ruffled his hair with her trunk. Beatrix laughed as he tried to flatten his messed up hair back down again.

'She does that to me all the time,' AJ said.

Tara made her *squee*ing trumpet sound.

'She sounds just like she's laughing when she makes that noise,' Yolanda said, shaking her head.

'Reminds me of a happy pig squeal,' Beatrix smiled.

'Beautiful day for the fete,' Mr Jones said.

'And a very special day,' said Mr Heelis.

'What's going to happen to Shanti and Tara now that the war's over?' Beatrix asked Mr Jones. 'Will they go back to the circus?'

'I hope not,' Mr Jones said. 'Thousands of people live peacefully side-by-side with elephants in Ceylon. There's no reason why we can't do so in Stony Oakhill.'

He'd written to Albert to offer him a job and a cottage on the farm, but Albert was still over in the Middle East and he hadn't heard back from him yet.

'I want them to stay here for ever,' said Yolanda.

'Me too,' said AJ.

'Stony Oakhill would be a much less interesting place without its elephants,' Annie said as she headed towards the fancy-dress parade wearing a long purple cloak.

'But they'll be taking the jobs of the horses,' said a man eating a hot pasty. A bit of it broke off and fell on the grass. Quick as a flash Harvey gobbled it up.

'When the horses come back, if any of them do ever get to come home, they deserve a jolly good feed and a long rest,' said a soldier with his arm in a sling. 'You haven't seen what they've been through, but I have.' And he shuddered at the horrific images in his head. 'Let the elephants do the horses' work for them for a little while. They've done enough.'

'Will Noodles and the horses come back soon?' Yolanda asked her dad. She was sure Tara, Shanti and Harvey would love her, and Buttercup and Bluebell, as much as she did.

'I hope so,' Mr Jones said, although he really didn't know.

Beatrix judged the best Herdwick sheep contest. But the judge for the fancy-dress competition hadn't arrived and Mr Jones was asked if he'd like to do it.

Mr Jones looked over at all the villagers in costume. Plus Annie and the other women from the Land Army who'd really gone to town with what little they could find up at the hostel. It was going to be very hard to judge.

'Why don't we let Shanti choose instead?' he said.

Everyone lined up and Shanti walked down the row of people in costume and back again.

She stopped at Annie, who was dressed as a queen with a wooden sceptre. She had an elaborate berry crown on her head, which Shanti proceeded to eat.

'I think we have a winner,' Mr Jones said and Annie was presented with the prize.

'I never usually win anything,' she said, her face beaming with delight.

'Did you hear that Houdini's touring again?' Beatrix asked her husband as Gwen, wearing her Sunday best clothes, sat down at an upright honky-tonk piano and started to play.

'Is he indeed?' said Mr Heelis. 'Well, I hope he won't be making an elephant vanish like he did in New York last year.'

'I don't think he'll be able to,' Beatrix smiled. 'He'd need a big venue like the Hippodrome to do that trick again.'

'Good. Having Tara go missing was more than enough for me. I don't want to see any other elephants vanish.'

Tara headed over to the sound of the music coming from the piano and Shanti followed her and watched as her daughter plonked her trunk on the keys to join in.

AJ pulled the harmonica from his pocket and headed over to Shanti.

'Here, Shanti. Show Tara what you can do,' he said, holding the harmonica out to her. Shanti blew on it with her trunk and, of course, Tara then wanted to have a go on that too.

For most people, the highlight of the day was the much anticipated football match between the villagers and the Land Army girls.

'Come on, Shanti,' AJ said, as he led her to her spot between the goal posts with the help of a carrot. Then he and Yolanda found a spot at the front of the crowd to watch the match.

Tara had picked up her long bunting ribbon again and was swinging it around when the whistle blew for the game to begin. When she and Harvey saw the ball and the players running after it they both raced to join in. Harvey might be old, but that didn't mean he didn't want to play or that he couldn't outrun the human footballers.

'Join in!' Annie shouted as she ran past AJ and Yolanda.

Yolanda pointed to herself and looked round. Surely she couldn't mean her.

'Yes, you!' Annie yelled.

And Yolanda laughed as she ran on to the pitch and went careering after the ball with the other women and girls from the WLA.

It was impossible to try and keep Shanti in goal because she wanted to chase after the ball too, and so the other players took it in turns to try and stop the ball from going into the net.

Tara had the ball and was running down the pitch pushing it in front of her with Harvey barking at her heels.

'That's it, Tara!' a familiar voice shouted.

At the sound of the voice, the little elephant stopped dead, raised her trunk, made her happy squee sound and ran to find its owner. Shanti came at a quick trundle behind her leaving the two teams looking confused.

'You're looking good, Shanti,' the stranger to the village said when the elephants reached him. Shanti raised her trunk and trumpeted loudly into the sky.

Harvey sniffed and whined. He hadn't smelt this smell for a long time and although it was different somehow from the way it used to be, underneath it was still the same. He ran towards the man as Yolanda watched him.

When all the animals reached Albert, Tara took off his hat with her trunk so she could ruffle his hair like she used to. Albert pressed his face against Shanti's and looked into her eyes. Then he crouched down to Harvey, who wagged his tail so hard it looked as if it might fall off, and all the time he gave little puppyish cries and licked Albert's face as if finally today all his wishes had come true.

The two elephants *squee*d and made rumbling sounds as if they were telling him all that had happened, whilst touching him gently with their trunks to welcome him home.

Yolanda and AJ came shyly forward, their father wheeling himself behind them. Annie came running over too, her face flushed from all the running about.

'You've looked after them so well, thank you,' Albert said, dashing away a tear so Annie wouldn't see it.

'I was wondering when we'd finally see you,' Annie said.

'You won't ever take them away, will you?' said AJ.

'We've got your cottage all ready for you,' said Yolanda.

Mr Jones grasped Albert's hand and shook it. 'There's a job here if you want it.'

'There's nowhere else I'd rather be.' Albert smiled. The Camel Corps had been disbanded in May, and as soon as it had been he'd left the Middle East and come home. All he wanted was to be with his animals, Shanti, Tara and Harvey, and he never ever wanted to go away again.

Epilogue

Albert was never the least bit tempted to go
back to the circus, especially when he saw how
much happier the elephants were now. Shanti
and Tara slept in the barn and came and went
as they liked. They had the farm to wander in
and the duck pond to bathe in, acres of forest
behind them and the Lake District in front.
The small cottage Mr Jones had given him was
perfect, but Albert didn't sleep in it most nights.
Instead he and Harvey slept in the barn with
the elephants.

There were so few horses now that Albert and Annie and the elephants were kept busy helping out on all the farms. If Albert needed the elephants to work and wasn't sure where they were he just rang a bell and they always came back. One day, six months after he'd come home from the war, the ringmaster came to see Albert, but he couldn't even get up the path to the cottage as Shanti, Tara and Harvey blocked his way.

'I'm thinking of starting the circus again if you're interested in signing up,' the ringmaster shouted from the gate to Albert. 'We used to make a good team.'

But Albert shook his head. The elephants and Harvey could perform at the village fete if they wanted to. Or just eat the apples people gave them anyway even if they didn't.

Yolanda and AJ were at Albert's cottage one June day when a gypsy caravan stopped at the gate. When she saw it, Tara immediately gave a delighted *squee* and went hurrying over to say hello. Harvey woke up from dozing in the sun and followed her, his tail wagging.

Tara touched Ezra, Sadie and their grandmother's hair gently with her trunk and squeed once again.

'She travelled on the road with us for a while,' Sadie explained to Albert, Yolanda and AJ. 'She and the dog.'

'Fed her some hay porridge mixed with honey, but what she really needed was her mum,' the grandmother said.

Ezra looked up at Shanti towering over them all and stretched out his hand to stroke her.

'I'm so glad she found you,' he said, as Harvey pushed his head under his hand for a stroke too.

Albert smiled. 'So you're the ones we have to thank,' he said. 'Without your kindness Tara probably wouldn't be alive. Are you staying in the village?'

Ezra shook his head. 'We pass this way going to or coming from the Appleby horse fair every year,' he told them.

'Then you should come back to see us every year,' Yolanda said, and AJ and Albert nodded as Ezra and Sadie grinned at each other.

'We will,' they said.

Harvey didn't follow Tara wherever she went now she had Shanti to watch over her. He liked to lie in the warm sunspot by the front door during the day when it was warm and next to Albert on the sofa, with his head resting on Albert's knee, when it wasn't.

'You're a good dog you are,' Albert said, as he stroked Harvey's old furry head and Harvey pressed his face to him. 'A very good dog indeed.'

From outside they could hear Shanti's gentle rumblings and Tara's happy trumpeting *squee*. Harvey's tail thumped up and down and he licked Albert's face.

Afterword

As soon as I heard about Lizzie the Sheffield elephant I knew I wanted to write a story about an elephant in the First World War. I decided to have my elephant helping on the home front and on a farm after reading in the newspaper archives about an elephant who went to live and work on a farm in 1901. The man bought the elephant at a circus auction and initially thought he would start his own circus with her. But when he found out how good she was at working on the farm he changed his mind. He never did start a circus, but he did keep the elephant, whom he described as gentle and docile.

When I started my research for this book I didn't know what a journey it would take me on as I discovered more and more about these amazing animals. I was horrified and appalled when I learnt about some of the cruel ways they've been treated and are still being treated today. But also uplifted and given hope by the many stories of human kindness and elephant awesomeness. All the things the elephants do in the book are based on the discoveries I made during my research.

I've taken liberties with some of the real life human characters who were around at the time. Beatrix Potter lived in Near Sawrey, close to Windermere, and was Mrs Heelis by 1917. In her journal and her letters to children she describes visiting the circus both in Scotland and the Lake District. She went on to publish *The Fairy Caravan* featuring a pigmy (pig dressed up) elephant. Edward Elgar was a great admirer of the Lake District, although, of course, he never met a piano-playing elephant there. And Harry Houdini did create a Vanishing Elephant trick, which was first performed in 1918.

The Appleby Horse Fair was granted a Royal Charter in 1685 and is still held each year in June at Appleby-in-Westmorland, Cumbria.

Acknowledgements

There are many people involved in making a book happen and be the best it can be possibly be. This one owes a debt of gratitude to a host of Puffins, including editors supreme Anthea Catchpole and Bella Pearson, copy-editors Samantha Stewart and Julia Bruce, cover designer and illustrator Richard Jones and Becky Morrison. On the PR side there's been Rhiannon Winfield and now Laura Smythe plus Jessica Farrugia-Sharples, marketing managers Gemma Rostill and Hannah Moloco, and sales sensations Tineke Mollemans and

Kirsty Bradbury. Not forgetting my lovely agent, Clare Pearson at Eddison Pearson.

As ever my dogs, Traffy and Bella, who were part of my book tour and made a brief appearance with me on stage at the Hay Festival, inspire all my work, keep me company on late-night writing bouts, accompany me on long walks and participate whenever possible in my research trips. Thanks to my brilliant husband being home whilst much of this book was written I was also able to leave the dogs in his caring hands whilst I headed out to do my research at places where dogs were not welcome.

Last, but by no means least, my heartfelt thanks must go to the many schoolchildren who responded so enthusiastically to my stories of Lizzie the Sheffield elephant and gave a resounding thumbs up to the idea of a book about an elephant on a farm in the First World War.

Here it is and I hope you enjoy it.

Have you read all Megan Rix's wonderful wartime animal stories?

'If you love Michael Morpurgo, you'll enjoy this' *Sunday Express*

AVAILABLE NOW

www.meganrix.com

Turn the page for an extract from

The Bomber Dog

by Megan Rix

AVAILABLE NOW

'A moving tale told with warmth, kindliness and lashings of good sense' *The Times*

Chapter 1

Close to the white cliffs of Dover, a little German Shepherd puppy cowered away from the seagulls that circled menacingly above him. He'd tried to run away from the birds but they were bigger and faster than he was. He'd barked at them but the seagulls' cries only seemed to mock his high puppy yap.

Molly, a honey-coated spaniel, spotted the puppy and the gulls near the docks. She barked and ran at the large, sharp-beaked birds, scattering them into the drizzly sky of the early February morning. The gulls dodged the silver barrage balloons that floated high in the air, and circled to land on the warships anchored in the harbour, screeching in protest. But they didn't return.

Once they'd gone, the rain-soaked, floppy-eared, sable-coated puppy came over to his rescuer, whimpering and trembling with fear and cold. Molly licked his blue-eyed face to reassure him and he nuzzled into her. His pitiful cries were gradually calming but his desperate hunger remained.

Molly used her nose to knock over a glass bottle of milk that the milkman had just left at the Dover harbour master's door. The bottle smashed and the puppy's little pink tongue lapped thirstily at the milk that flowed on to the ground.

'Get away from that!' the milkman yelled angrily, when he saw the puppy drinking. His boot kicked out at him, only narrowly missing the puppy's little legs. Molly barked at the milkman and she and the pup ran off together with the milkman's furious shouts still ringing in their ears.

The smell of the sea and the reek of the oil from the ships grew fainter as they ran, but the small dog wasn't strong enough to run for very long yet, and they slowed to a walk as soon as they left the docks. Molly led the puppy through the outskirts of Dover to her den, a derelict garden shed at the edge of the allotments. There was sacking on the floor, it had a solid waterproof roof, and as an added bonus, every now and again a foolish rat or mouse would enter the shed – only to be pounced on and eagerly gulped down.

The tired puppy sank down on the sacking and immediately fell fast asleep, exhausted from the morning's excitement. Britain was in the grip of the Second World War, and Dover was a crucially important port, constantly filled with the hustle and bustle of ships and soldiers, but the puppy was blissfully unaware of all that.

Molly lay down too, her head resting on her paws, but she didn't sleep; she watched over her new companion.

Only a few weeks ago, Molly had been a much-loved pet, until a bomb had hit the house she lived in.

She remembered her owner being put on a stretcher and rushed to hospital, but Molly herself hadn't been found. She'd stayed hidden amid the rubble, shaking uncontrollably, too traumatized to make a sound.

She'd stayed in exactly the same spot for the rest of the night, covered in debris, too scared to sleep. At dawn she'd crawled out of her hiding place and taken her first tentative steps towards the shattered window and the world outside, alone.

The puppy snuffled in his sleep and Molly licked him gently until he settled. There were hundreds, maybe thousands, of lost and abandoned dogs in Dover but at least she and this baby Alsatian had found each other.

For the first few weeks, the puppy stayed as close to Molly as he could, never allowing the two of them to get more than a few steps apart. Wherever she went he followed her, not wanting to be left alone again, even for a moment.

Every night they lay close together on the sacking and kept each other warm, listening to the bomber planes as they flew overhead on their way to London and other cities.

As the weeks turned into months, and winter turned into spring and then summer, the bomber planes and the bombs they dropped became so commonplace that they no longer woke Molly or her young friend, curled up together in the shed.

Now one year old, the German Shepherd

was no longer the vulnerable puppy he'd once been, but Molly still licked his furry sable head to soothe him when he twitched and cried out in his sleep. He still had the same piercing blue eyes he'd had as a young puppy, but one of his ears now stood straight up, while the other still flopped down. With Molly's care and love he'd grown fast and he was now much larger and stronger than her, but she was still definitely the leader of their two-dog pack.

Their first priority each day was always to find food – and the most delicious food in the world, just waiting for a dog to help himself, was in the pig bins.

Two or more tin dustbins were set on most street corners for people's waste food. These dustbins were collected every week and taken out to farms to feed the pigs. Although the bins were emptied regularly, they still attracted flies, especially in the warm summer weather.

Molly and the German Shepherd didn't

mind about the bluebottles that buzzed around the bins. In fact, the young dog sometimes forgot the reason they'd come to the pig bins in his excitement at trying to catch one. He'd jump and snap at the insects as they flew out of the pig bins and buzzed around him, almost taunting him, daring him to try and catch them. He did dare, but however hard he tried, he only occasionally managed to swallow one.

Molly would remind him with a look or a whine, and occasionally even a bark, that they were at the pig bins to eat. Then he would stick his head in the bin and gorge himself until he could eat no more. Sometimes the leftovers had only just been put in the bin and were fresh, but more often, if the bins hadn't been emptied in the previous few days, they were rancid and mouldy. The dogs ate them anyway, ate and ate and ate.

Today, Molly led her young friend to two

bins at the bottom of a dead-end street. He skilfully knocked the lid off the first one and then sneezed with excitement at the tantalizing smell coming from inside it. The next moment all that could be seen of him was a fiercely wagging tail as his sensitive nose investigated the intriguing scent coming from the bottom of the bin. He was so busy trying to reach it that he didn't even hear the growl.

But Molly did. She turned to find five vicious-looking feral dogs spoiling for a fight. The growl had come from their leader: a large rough-furred, yellow-toothed, muscular dog that towered menacingly over Molly.

Molly gave a low, warning growl in return.

It was at this moment that the German Shepherd emerged, triumphant, to show Molly what he'd found. The ham bone had been right at the bottom of the bin, and old potato peelings and cabbage leaves dropped from him as he rose. He hadn't expected to find five snarling dogs waiting for him. The brutish-looking leader drooled at the sight of the bone.

The dogs' faces twisted into snarls as they headed towards him. There was only one way out – he leapt from the pig bin and raced past them and out on to the main street. The feral dogs turned and charged after him, while Molly ran after them, barking loudly.

He raced down one street, and up another, and still they followed him. They were big dogs and looked better fed than him, but he was much quicker.

The large ham bone was heavy in his mouth and slippery in his jaws, but he wouldn't let it go, not even when one of the pack got so close he could hear it breathing. He doubled back through an alleyway, dodged left then twisted right, racing on through the graveyard, and back through a concealed hole in the fence and into the allotments, where he hid in the blackberry bushes. He panted as he listened intently for the sound of the other dogs, but there was nothing. He'd successfully lost them and he gnawed on his ham bone trophy with relish.

Molly found him a few minutes later and came up to him, out of breath. He dropped the bone and nudged it over to her with his nose. She wagged her tail in thanks and gnawed on it. The bone had been worth it and they took it in turns to chew on it until it was quite gone.

At twilight they made their way back to their den in the old disused shed.

The blackout had been in force since the beginning of the war, so with no street lights on and with clouds hiding the stars, it grew very dark very quickly.

Usually the young dog paid very little attention to the high wailing sound of the air-raid siren.

It was such a common noise, one he'd heard since he was born and he, like many other pets, knew instinctively when no bomber planes were headed in their direction and there was nothing to fear.

But tonight was different. Tonight the hackles along his back rose and he sat up and listened to the strange, almost bird-like whistling sound. Tonight he was afraid. He got to his feet but there wasn't time to run before the bomb fell. A deafening roar filled his ears and for a moment the whole world seemed to collapse around him. The force of the blast threw him across the shed, and he lay still as the dusty air swirled about him.

For a moment he was knocked out, but as soon as he came to, he belly-crawled over to Molly who lay unconscious on the ground.

He whined and nuzzled his head against hers but her eyes didn't open. He lay down beside her to keep her warm and listened as outside in the street people called to each other, fire-engine bells rang and ambulances screeched to a halt.

Then he smelt a new smell. The smell of smoke. A spark from the burning houses had fallen on the shed and now it began to smoulder.

The dog whined again and then barked at Molly, but still she didn't stir. He pawed at his friend, instinctively knowing that the smell meant serious danger.

In desperation he barked again and then he took hold of Molly's collar with his teeth and pulled. Although Molly was much smaller than he was it was still almost impossible for him to drag her leaden body across the uneven ground. He lost his grip, whined, then gripped her collar more firmly in his teeth and crouched low so he could pull her with every ounce of strength he had.

The back wall of the shed had been completely blown away in the blast and he dragged Molly out of it and across the ground away from the flames that had now taken hold. Then he lay down beside her in the smoke and ash-filled air, panting and trembling.

Molly was in a bad way; her fur was coated in blood and her breathing was ragged. The anxious young dog licked his friend's face and whimpered.

Turn the page for an extract from

The Great Escape

by Megan Rix

AVAILABLE NOW

www.meganrix.com

Chapter 1

On a steamy hot Saturday morning in the summer of 1939, a Jack Russell with a patch of tan fur over his left eye and a black spot over his right was digging as though his life depended upon it.

His little white forepaws attacked the soft soil, sending chrysanthemums, stocks and freesias to their deaths. He'd soon dug so deep that the hole was bigger than he was, and all that could be seen were sprays of flying soil and his fiercely wagging tail.

'Look at Buster go,' twelve-year-old Robert Edwards said, leaning on his spade. 'He could win a medal for his digging.'

Robert's best friend, Michael, laughed. 'Bark when you reach Australia!' he told Buster's rear end. He tipped the soil from his shovel on to the fast-growing mound beside them.

Buster's tail wagged as he emerged from the hole triumphant, his muddy treasure gripped firmly in his mouth.

'Oh no, better get that off him!' Robert said, when he realized what Buster had.

'What is it?' Michael asked.

'One of Dad's old slippers – he's been looking for them everywhere.'

'But how did it get down there?'

Buster cocked his head to one side, his right ear up and his left ear down.

'*Someone* must have buried it there. Buster – give!'

But Buster had no intention of giving up his treasure. As Robert moved closer to him Buster danced backwards.

'Buster – Buster – give it to me!'

Robert and Michael raced around the garden after Buster, trying to get the muddy, chewed slipper from him. Buster thought this was a wonderful new game of chase, and almost lost the slipper by barking with excitement as he dodged this way and that.

The game got even better when Robert's nine-year-old sister Lucy, and Rose the collie, came out of the house and started to chase him too.

'Buster, come back . . .'

Rose tried to circle him and cut him off. Until recently she'd been a sheepdog and she was much quicker than Buster, but he managed to evade her by jumping over the ginger-and-white cat, Tiger, who wasn't pleased to be used as a fence and hissed at Buster to tell him so.

Buster was having such a good time. First digging

up the flower bed, now playing chase. It was the perfect day – until Lucy dived on top of him and he was trapped.

'Got you!'

Robert took Dad's old slipper from Buster. 'Sorry, but you can't play with that.'

Buster jumped up at the slipper, trying to get it back. It was his – he'd buried it and he'd dug it up. Robert held the slipper above his head so Buster couldn't get it, although for such a small dog, he could jump pretty high.

Buster went back to his hole and started digging to see if he could find something else interesting. Freshly dug soil was soon flying into the air once again.

'No slacking, you two!' Robert's father, Mr Edwards, told the boys as he came out of the back door. Robert quickly hid the slipper behind him; he didn't want Buster to get into trouble. Michael took it from him, unseen.

Lucy ran back into the kitchen, with Rose close behind her.

'You two should be following Buster's example,' Mr Edwards said to the boys.

At the sound of his name Buster stopped digging for a moment and emerged from his hole. His face was covered in earth and it was clear that he was in his element. Usually he'd have been in huge trouble for digging in the garden, but not today. When

Mr Edwards wasn't looking, Michael dropped the slipper into the small ornamental fishpond near to where Tiger was lying. Tiger rubbed his head against Michael's hand, the bell on his collar tinkling softly, and Michael obligingly stroked him behind his ginger ears before getting back to work.

Tiger had been out on an early-morning prowl of the neighbourhood when the government truck had arrived and the men from it had rung the doorbell of every house along the North London terraced street. Each homeowner had been given six curved sheets of metal, two steel plates and some bolts for fixing it all together.

'There you go.'

'Shouldn't take you more than a few hours.'

'Got hundreds more of these to deliver.'

Four of the workmen helped those who couldn't manage to put up their own Anderson Shelters, but everyone else was expected to dig a large hole in their back garden, deep enough so that only two feet of the six-foot-high bomb shelter could be seen above the ground.

Buster, Robert and Michael had set to work as soon as they'd been given theirs, with Mr Edwards supervising.

'Is the hole big enough yet, Dad?' Robert asked his father. They'd been digging for ages.

Mr Edwards peered at the government instruction leaflet and shook his head. 'It needs to be four foot deep in the soil. And we'll need to dig steps down to the door.'

Tiger surveyed the goings-on through half-closed eyes from his favourite sunspot on the patio. He was content to watch as Buster wore himself out and got covered in mud. It was much too hot a day to do anything as energetic as digging.

In the kitchen, Rose was getting in the way as usual.

'Let me past, Rose,' said Lucy and Robert's mother, Mrs Edwards, turning away from the window.

Rose took a step or two backwards, but she was still in the way. The Edwardses' kitchen was small, but they'd managed to cram a wooden dresser as well as two wooden shelves and a cupboard into it. It didn't have a refrigerator.

'What were you all doing out there?' Mrs Edwards asked Lucy.

Lucy thought it best not to mention that Buster had dug up Dad's old slipper. It was from Dad's favourite pair and Mum had turned the house upside-down searching for it.

'Just playing,' she said.

Lucy began squeezing six lemon halves into a brown earthenware jug while her mother made sugar syrup by adding a cup of water and a cup of sugar to a saucepan and bringing it to the boil on the coal gas stove. Wearing a full-length apron over her button-down dress, Mrs Edwards stirred continuously so as not to scorch the syrup or the pan.

The letterbox rattled and Lucy went to see what it was. Another government leaflet lay on the mat. They seemed to be getting them almost every day now. This one had 'Sand to the Rescue' written in big letters and gave instructions on how to place sandbags so that they shielded the windows, and how to dispose of incendiary bombs using a sand-bucket and scoop.

Lucy put the leaflet on the dresser with the others and went to check on her cakes. She didn't want them to burn, especially not with Michael visiting.

Two hours later Mr Edwards declared, 'That should be enough.'

Robert and Michael stopped digging and admired their work. Buster, however, wasn't ready to stop yet. He wanted them to dig a second, even bigger hole, and he knew exactly where that hole should be. His little paws got busy digging in the new place.

'No, Buster, no more!' Robert said firmly.

Buster stopped and sat down. He watched as Robert, Michael and Mr Edwards assembled the Anderson Shelter from the six corrugated iron sheets and end plates, which they bolted together at the top.

'Right, that's it, easy does it,' Mr Edwards told the boys. The Anderson Shelter was up and in place.

For the first time Tiger became interested. The

shelter looked like a new choice sunspot – especially when the sun glinted on its corrugated iron top. He uncurled himself and sauntered over to it.

'Hello, Tiger. Come to have a look?' Michael asked him. Tiger ignored the question, jumped on to the top of the shelter and curled up on the roof.

Robert and Michael laughed. 'He must be the laziest cat in the world,' Robert said. 'All he does is eat and sleep and then sleep again.'

Tiger's sunbathing was cut short.

'You can't sleep there, Tiger,' Mr Edwards said. 'And we can't have the roof glinting in the sunshine like that. Go on – scat, cat.'

Tiger ran a few feet away and then stopped and watched as Mr Edwards and the boys now shovelled the freshly dug soil pile they'd made back on top of the roof of the bomb shelter, with Buster trying to help by digging at the pile – which wasn't really any help at all.

Mr Edwards wiped his brow as he stopped to look at the instruction leaflet again. 'It says it needs to be covered with at least fifteen inches of soil above the roof,' he told Robert and Michael.

The three of them kept on shovelling until the shelter was completely hidden by the newly dug soil.

Lucy and Mrs Edwards came out, carrying freshly made lemonade and fairy cakes.

'Good, we've earned this,' Robert said when he saw them.

'Those look very appetizing, Lucy love,' Mr Edwards said when Lucy held out the plate of cakes.

'Do you like it?' Lucy asked Michael, as he bit into his cake. Her eyes were shining.

'Delicious,' Michael smiled, and took another bite.

Buster was desperate to taste one of Lucy's cakes too. He looked at her meaningfully, mouth open, tail wagging winningly. When that didn't work he tried sitting down and lifting his paws in the air in a begging position.

Lucy furtively nudged one of the cakes off the plate on to the ground.

'Oops!'

Buster was on it and the cake was gone in one giant gulp. He looked up hopefully for more.

Mr Edwards took a long swig of his lemonade and put his beaker back on the tray. 'So, what do you think?' he asked his wife.

Mrs Edwards's flower garden was ruined. 'It's going to make it very awkward to hang out the weekly washing.'

'In a few weeks' time even I'd have trouble spotting it from the air,' Mr Edwards said. He was a reconnaissance pilot and was used to navigating from landmarks on the ground. 'It'll be covered in weeds and grass and I bet we could even grow flowers or tomato plants on it if we wanted to.'

Lucy grinned. 'But you'd still know we were nearby and wave to us from your plane, wouldn't you, Dad?'

'I would,' smiled Mr Edwards. 'With Alexandra Palace just round the corner, our street is hard to miss. But Jerry flying over with his bombs won't have a clue the Anderson Shelter's down here with you hidden inside it – and that's the main thing.'

Lucy shivered. 'Will there really be another war, Dad?' It was a question everyone was asking.

'I hope not. I really do,' Mr Edwards said, putting his arm round his wife. 'They called the last one the Great War and told us it was the war to end all wars. But now that looks doubtful.'

Michael helped himself to another of Lucy's cakes and smiled at her.

Lucy was beaming as she went back inside, with Rose following her.

As Lucy filled Buster's bowl with fresh water and took it back outside, Rose padded behind her like a shadow. She chose different people, and occasionally Buster or Tiger, to follow on different days. But she chose Lucy most of all. She'd tried to herd Buster and Tiger once or twice, as she used to do with the sheep, but so far this hadn't been very successful, due to Buster and Tiger's lack of cooperation.

'Here, Buster, you must be thirsty too after all that digging,' Lucy said, putting his water bowl down on the patio close to Tiger, who stretched out his legs and flexed his sharp claws. Lucy stroked him and Tiger purred.

Buster lapped at the water with his little pink tongue.

'Buster deserves a bone for all that digging,' Robert said. 'Or at least a biscuit or two.'

Buster looked up at him and wagged his tail.

'Go on then,' Mrs Edwards said.

Robert went inside and came back with Buster's tin of dog biscuits. Buster wagged his tail even more enthusiastically at the sight of the tin, and wolfed down the biscuit Robert gave him. Bones or biscuits – food was food.

'Here, Rose, want a biscuit?' Robert asked her.

Rose accepted one and then went to lie down beside the bench on which Lucy was sitting. She preferred it when everyone was together in the same place; only then could she really settle.

Just a few months ago Rose had been living in Devon and working as a sheepdog. But things had changed when the elderly farmer didn't come out one morning, or the next. Rose waited for the farmer at the back door from dawn to dusk and then went back to the barn where she slept. But the farmer never came.

Some days the farmer's wife brought a plate of food for her. Some days she forgot and Rose went to sleep hungry.

Then the farmer's daughter, Mrs Edwards, came to the farm, dressed in black, and the next day she took Rose back to London with her on the train. Rose never saw the farmer again.

Rose whined and Lucy bent and stroked her head.

'Feeling sad?' she asked her.

Sometimes Rose had a faraway look in her eyes that made Lucy wonder just what Rose was thinking. Did she miss Devon? It must be strange for Rose only having a small garden to run about in when she was used to herding sheep with her grandfather on the moor.

'Do you miss Grandad?'

Rose licked Lucy's hand.

'I miss him too,' Lucy said.

When they all went back indoors, Tiger stayed in the garden. He took a step closer to the Anderson Shelter and then another step and another. Tiger was a very curious sort of cat, and being shooed away had only made him more curious. He ran down the earth steps and peered into the new construction.

Inside it was dark, but felt cool and slightly damp after the heat of the sun.

'Tiger!' Lucy called, coming back out. 'Tiger, where are you?'

Lucy came down the garden and found him.

'There you are. Why didn't you come when I called you?' She picked Tiger up like a baby, with his paws waving in the air, and carried him out of the shelter and back up to the house. It wasn't the most comfortable or dignified way of travelling, but Tiger put up with it because it was Lucy. Ever since Tiger had arrived at the Edwardses' house as a tiny mewling kitten, he and Lucy had had a special bond.

They stopped at the living room where Robert was showing Michael Buster's latest trick.

'Slippers, Buster,' Robert said.

Buster raced to the shoe rack by the front door, found Robert's blue leather slippers and raced back with one of them in his mouth. He dropped the slipper beside Robert.

Robert put his foot in it and said, 'Slippers,' again. Buster raced off and came back with the other one.

Robert gave him a dog biscuit.

Michael grinned. 'He's so smart.'

'He can identify Dad and Mum and Lucy's slippers too,' Robert told Michael. He'd decided not to risk Dad's new slippers with Buster today. 'You're one clever dog, aren't you, Buster?'

Buster wagged his tail like mad and then raced round and round, chasing it.

'Tiger and Rose can do tricks too,' Lucy said, putting Tiger down in an armchair. 'And Rose doesn't need to be bribed with food to do them. Look – down, Rose.'

Rose obediently lay down.

Lucy moved across the room and Rose started to stand up to follow her.

'Stay, Rose.'

Rose lay back down again.

'Good girl.'

'So what tricks can Tiger do?' Michael asked Lucy.

Lucy pulled a strand of wool from her mum's knitting basket and waggled it in front of Tiger like a snake wriggling around the carpet. Tiger jumped off the armchair, stalked the wool and captured it with his paw.

Tail held high, he went over to Robert and then to Michael to allow them the honour of stroking him.

Tiger didn't need tricks to be admired.